MURDER ON
THE DODDER

Also by Keith Bruton

The Lemon Man

MURDER ON THE DODDER

KEITH BRUTON

BRASH
BOOKS

ISBN-13: 978-1-954841-76-5

Brash Books
PO Box 8212
Calabasas, CA 91372
www.brash-books.com

For Rachel, always

We are all born mad. Some remain so.

Samuel Beckett, *Waiting for Godot*

TO-DO LIST

MOUNT JEROME CEMETERY

PENNEYS

GREGORY'S IRONWORKS

BAGGOT STREET

CHAPTER ONE

I see the O'Donovan Rossa Bridge to my right and get a move on. I hear someone singing "The Lovely Sweet Banks of the Moy" into a microphone. It's about a fifteen-minute cycle to my destination.

My legs are sweating in these trousers as I make my way down the paths. I miss me shorts. I come up to Winetavern Street. To my left is the glorious Christ Church Cathedral, founded circa 1030. The building is enormous, impressive at every angle and for any visitor, a must-have photo for the collection.

As I cycle under a charming arch, I feel my belly growl. I skipped breakfast this morning. I'm fasting. I'm trying to lose a few pounds. I haven't cycled in weeks. My body should be brand-new, but I feel sluggish and jaded.

Patrick Street. It's a straight road all the way to Harold's Cross. Not much to see on these streets. Old redbrick houses and apartments. I stop at a red light. The smell of fresh bread lingers from the bakery across from me. My mouth salivates.

A round plaque on an enchanting house reads **HERE, IN JOYCE'S IMAGINATION WAS BORN IN MAY 1866 LEOPOLD BLOOM.**

A car beeps its horn at me. The light turns green. I'm off. I pedal faster, flying over Emmet Bridge, mouth gaping like an alligator.

I reach Harold's Cross on time. I jump off my bike, lock it to a railing, and head through the dainty park, which is the shape of a triangle.

I hear loud screaming of sorts to my far right. There's a playground full of joyful children chasing one another in colorful clothing and a café with a mob of boomers smoking outside, yapping away as they drink their foamy lattes and eat buttery croissants.

A border collie races after a tennis ball across a patch of green grass to my left that looks like a crop circle. I walk around it and get to the other side of the park. I catch a glimpse of a whimsical waterfall. Not far from the rockery is a Little Free Library. A hardback of Ian Fleming's *Casino Royale* is poking out between a Jamie Oliver cookbook and a book on yoga.

Mount Jerome Cemetery is across the road. Outside the main entrance is a Ford van, the color deep blue, with many dents. I cross the road and a tanned woman in her sixties with gold jewelry around her neck is selling dozens of colorful flowers dunked in large pots. I snatch the cheapest bunch of flowers, yellow tulips wrapped in white paper that cost a fiver.

Before I enter the gates of hell, I notice the pavements are smeared with pigeon droppings and chewing gum is glued to the ground. I scratch my chest. The shirt feels like the new bedsheets I put on yesterday. To my left is the Church of the Holy Apostles Peter and Paul.

I stroll into Mount Jerome Cemetery. The intimidating gates are tall and spiky and have haunting pillars on either side. I get a nippy chill down my back as I enter. I keep moving, holding the tulips in my hand. Water drips from the stems, making my wrist and shirt wet.

The road is narrow, with thick trees on both sides, the type of trees you would see deep in the woodlands. There are sporadic sounds of agitated blackbirds rustling in the branches high above.

The bells go off at Mount Jerome Victorian Chapel, not too far ahead of me. I remember the chapel having high vaulted wooden ceilings, hideous red carpet, and the distinctive scent of beeswax and incense. The cemetery is quite extraordinary the farther I go in.

It's almost fifty acres, with its first burial in 1836. Now it holds over three hundred thousand burials. So many headstones, so much crumbling concrete. A gray landscape giving a bleak atmosphere, which makes me feel queasy and depressed.

Big names are cremated or buried here. They include playwright John Millington Synge, beloved writer Maeve Binchy, Oscar Wilde's father, William, painter Jack Butler Yeats, and Ireland's most notorious criminal Martin "The General" Cahill.

I stop for a second or two and look out at the sea of gray slabs. I remove my notebook from my back pocket, lick my thumb, and flick through the pages. I land on a page with a badly drawn map of the cemetery. Now there's ink on my fingertips. I stare at the smudged map. I have to be careful. The place is like a maze. One wrong turn and I'm done for.

I make a right. I move at a good pace on the stones, which make a crispy, crunchy sound. Some cemeteries might have healthy grass on top of the graves, but not this one. Melancholy is in the air as death surrounds me. I scan the headstones and glance at the dates. A lot of young deaths back in the day, children and babies. I see a grave with a flashy blue balloon, half-deflated, blowing in the wind. The grave beside it has cans of Druids Celtic Cider on it.

A miniature temple consisting of a large three-tier granite base is up ahead. Ten Tuscan columns support an entablature. Truly breathtaking. The name **CUSACK** is engraved on the structure. It looks out of place, like it belongs in the Roman Forum.

I swing a hard left and walk straight. I count twenty-two headstones. I stop. I see a taxi crawling out on the far side of the cemetery. Dead silence. Nobody about. Beyond the walls are houses. It's not the most pleasant view from their back windows.

I see a headstone and quickly take a knee to hide. I place the tulips on the grave and walk away. I look at my map again. I have a drawing of an angel. I look up and see the female angel praying a couple of rows deep in the cemetery. Her head is camouflaged in moss. I walk toward her, moving a little faster.

I stop and glance up at the pretty statue. Beside the grave is a hole six feet deep. I lean forward. Nothing inside. I look at the time on my phone and hear the sound of crunching footsteps behind me. I put my phone away and slip on my leather gloves. The scent of tulips tickles my nose hairs, causing my nostrils to flare.

Four headstones away is an older man, in his mid-sixties, gray hair, plump, with a saggy face like a bloodhound. Even his eyelids are droopy. He glances at me. I take a few steps over to him, my hands behind my back.

"Bit of a chilly breeze this morning," I say.

"Yeah, there is," he replies, calmly turning his head back to the grave. His hands are folded together as if I've interrupted his praying. He's wearing a beige rain jacket and a pair of battered blue jeans you'd see in a charity shop. His white trainers have dirt on the bottom of them.

"It's one of those days where I could just sit in all day, put the fireplace on, and listen to old records with a warm cuppa or maybe some hot chocolate," I say with a thin smile. "I did that last weekend... I had the place to myself and spent hours listening to the same record over and over again. Joy Division's *Unknown Pleasures*. Classic album. You got to say, when it's all said and done and we talk about the greats who have done it... Stones, Beatles, Zeppelin, Pink Floyd, and so on. Joy Division will be standing beside them lot on top of the mountain... without question."

He doesn't respond or even acknowledge me. He just stares at the headstone in front of him. So I keep talking.

"I'm tellin' ye, *Unknown Pleasures* is a masterpiece. Feckin' stunning debut album, wouldn't ye say? I think so... The record is chilling to the bone, almost as haunting as this bloody cemetery we are standing in this lovely morning," I say, adjusting my gloves.

"The lead singer, Ian Curtis, was unbelievable... what a tortured soul, wasn't he? Talk about traumatic." I shake my shoulders as if I'm possessed with the shivers. "Don't get me wrong, I did like their second record, *Closer*. Ye know, it was ambitious, but the fucker should have just ended his life after the first one. It would have been the perfect send-off album before he hanged himself with a bleedin' washing line. Don't leave us with *Closer*, please for the love of God, don't leave us with fuckin' *Closer!*"

"Stop! Stop it!" the man barks back at me. As he turns to face me, he starts grinding his teeth and trembling. I remove the Glock 17 from the back of my trousers and screw the silencer on behind my back.

"Ian Curtis." I say the name and his face turns red. "I heard that's what you've changed your name to these days. What did the papers used to call ye? Oh, I remember, Connor 'The Savage' Dunphy, the man who tied up his wife, gagged, and raped her. Followed by stabbing her in the head with a corkscrew."

"Shut up!"

"Then you dismembered her body with a hacksaw. Discarding her body parts at the local dump. Some fuckin' husband you turned out to be."

"That wasn't me," he bellows out. Tears fill his eyes, making them shiny.

"Dirty, rotten bastard!" I yell at him. "The night you butchered your wife, the neighbors recalled hearing loud music being played... *Unknown Pleasures* on repeat, they said. Over and over and over a—"

"It was someone else, I promise. He told me to do it," he says, smacking his skull with both hands.

"Eleven scabby years for slaughtering your wife like she was nothing. And the audacity to go by the name of the great Ian Curtis. Now the kids have no mother or fuckin' father."

I extend my right arm out, aiming the gun at him. He opens his mouth wordlessly, terror in his eyes.

His day has arrived.

I press the trigger three times, hitting his chest with precision. He falls on his knees, then flat on his face.

I walk over to his dead body lying on the sharp stones and put another two bullets in the cunt's head. The silencer is still warm. I unscrew it and put it in my pocket. I quickly drag his dead body to the hole behind me and roll his body in. He drops, landing on his back, arms down by his sides. There's a temptation to spit on him, but he's not worth it. I need to move quickly.

I kick the bullet shells into the hole. I turn my head and watch a white dump truck come around the corner, striking a few limp branches, almost snapping them off. I can hear its tires on the stones as it approaches me.

It stops two feet away from me. The driver's door flings open. An older woman emerges. She is about seventy years old. She comes walking toward me wearing a red flannel shirt, blue jeans, and rubber boots. She stands next to me, and we both look down into the deep hole.

"Isn't that a pleasant sight?" she says. Half of her face is lopsided from a stroke. She looks as if she's growling.

She gets back in the truck and reverses it toward the hole. She presses a button and the truck's box inclines high. Fresh soil spills out from the back like coffee grounds, filling up the hole in a matter of seconds.

"Grab a shovel," she says out the window.

We both spend the next five minutes making sure the dirt is leveled out properly. The heavy clouds above us turn dark gray. "Why are ye called the Lemon Man?" she asks me. "Peculiar name, isn't it?"

My eyes fixate on the dirt as my mind brings me back ten years ago to my first ever hit in Carrickmines, on the outskirts of Dublin. I remember it clearly. Standing nervously in a stuffy greenhouse, disguised as a gardener. My hands were trembling and clammy, and the sweat was sliding down my forehead onto my nose.

Then it happened. The former Lord Mayor of Dublin turned around, my eyes widened, and I raised my arm and shot him in the neck. I watched him choke on his own blood, then put him out of his misery with a shot to the back of the head. Moments before I killed him, he said sternly to me, "You must be the lemon man." The name has stuck with me ever since.

But I couldn't tell her that. Instead, I hand her an envelope with two hundred euros inside. She takes the envelope from me, nods, and walks away. She knows the deal. She's done this a million times. I'm all damp and filthy. I wipe my black trousers, which doesn't even make a bloody difference.

I remove my notebook, crossing off my first task of the day. Job done. As I leave the cemetery, I catch a glimpse of the yellow tulips on the grave. The tiny headstone simply reads **IN LOVING MEMORY OF TREASA CALLEN, 1950–2022.**

~~MOUNT JEROME CEMETERY~~

CHAPTER TWO

It's a perfect day for a bit of cycling in the city of Dublin. I need to play something relaxing to calm the mind down. I still have a bit of head rush after killing Connor "The Savage" Dunphy. What a sick bastard he was.

Every year the prisons release a dozen or so killers back onto the streets. The average life sentence is about eighteen years. Not much of a life sentence. That's where I come in. I get paid to kill these scumbags. I've been a hit man for ten years and that's what pays the bills. It's no nine-to-five job, far from it, but I'm the best in the country at it.

Now, ask yourself the question, if someone close to you got hurt, abused, or murdered by some lowlife, wouldn't you want them dead?

I wasn't alone on my first ever hit. Guiding me through an earpiece was Danny Murphy, aka Eagle Eye, one of the deadliest men with a sniper rifle. His pinpoint accuracy is known across Europe. He showed me how to stalk prey and kill it swiftly. You could say he was my mentor. Things didn't end well between us the last time we spoke. Let's just say a heist didn't go according to plan.

My headphones are in my ears. I press on the song "Experience" by Ludovico Einaudi on my phone. The sound of Einaudi's fingers playing the piano soothes the tension around my head.

I cycle patiently along the enchanting canal—well, parts of it are. It's 132 kilometers, so you're going to have a few sketchy parts, but all in all it's peaceful, even hypnotic.

I once saw a supermarket trolley floating in the canal. How does a feckin' shopping trolley end up there? Did some troubled children steal it from a supermarket car park and when they got bored playing with it, they flung it in the canal? Or was it a homeless person who just had enough of pushing their shit around the city and said the hell with it, this is going swimming with the swans?

The greenish-brown canal begins at the river Liffey and goes through the river Shannon, the longest river in Ireland. It's a smooth ride for me in the bike lane. Well, sort of. Dodging potholes, overgrown branches, and tipped-over traffic cones is expected. And not to forget, those bloody food-delivery riders on their expensive electric bikes. They always overtake me on the road.

The music in my ears is spellbinding. I feel like I'm in a trance. I make a smooth left over the La Touche Bridge in Portobello.

A gentleman at the post office once told me a terrible tragedy that occurred on the bridge. He was a scrawny man with a black head of hair that looked dyed. He told me back in the day a man was driving a horse-bus up over the bridge and one of the horses reared violently, causing the bus to go through the rails of the bridge. Everyone fell over, landing in the murky waters below. All six passengers died. He didn't blink once as he told me the story, just gazed into my eyes like a madman.

I'd only asked him for the bloody time.

Richmond Street. For once I get green lights all the way to Dame Street. The city is lively. I continue to cycle, passing the magnificent Bank of Ireland building to my left. They always put a gigantic Christmas tree outside the main entrance, with bright lights, in the month of December.

Facing Trinity College is a statue of orator Henry Grattan with one hand clinging to the lapel of his jacket and one hand up heroically to the sky.

I turn sharply on Westmoreland Street and head over O'Connell Bridge. It's a busy Saturday. I wait for the tram to pass me by. The monument of "the Liberator," Daniel O'Connell, is high above me as I head up on the path. Hopping off, I lock me bike around a tree.

It probably isn't the safest place to leave my bike, but I was only going to be a few minutes. I look down to see I have grease smeared all over my suit trousers. I'm so used to wearing shorts on the bike, I forget that grease from the chain can get on your clothing. It's why you see so many hipsters rolling their socks over their trousers.

I cross the road, turning off my music. Eason's bookstore is a five-story building. The bronze plaque over the entrance dates it to 1919. It's has a suspended square-plan clock with a gilt face outside the main door. Each floor has sliding sash windows and for the ground floor, polished granite pilasters and Doric columns.

But that isn't the building I'll be entering. It will be the one next door. In a light-sea-green font above the entrance is the word **PENNEYS**, known for its low-priced clothing and the barbarians who shop inside. It's been a while since I last made a visit to this store. I trudge on in.

The Middle Eastern chap working as security is standing stiff like a cardboard cutout as I enter. His displeased facial expression gazes at me up and down.

The bottom floor of the store is madness. It's the women's section. Women of all ages and colors use their claws to latch on to everything, dropping pieces of clothing on the floor and not picking them up.

Stampeding from aisle to aisle, they're holding on to too much shit. A basket rolls over my foot and there's a stuffy odor in the air of bitter perfumes and the musky stench of sweat, like I'm inside a men's changing room after a football match.

To my right, a child of about five with his arms covered in freckles is about to cry. He starts to fret.

"What's wrong, young man?" I ask the poor thing.

"I can't find me ma," he replies sobbing.

"I'm sure we can find her," I say.

A heavyset woman with bleached-blond hair and arched dark brows comes rushing over to the boy.

"What did I fuckin' tell ye about running off," she yells at the boy with a mouthful of chipped teeth. She grabs him viciously by the arm, hauling him through the aisle like he's a basket. His feet drag along the floor like wheels.

I go up the second floor using the escalator. I reach the top and I overhear an American woman say, "Isn't this place just fantastic." Her accent sounds southern.

I make my way over to the men's section. I pick up a plain black T-shirt for three euro. Then I go over to the summer clothing, even though it's spring. Three Portuguese-speaking fellas try on flashy blue trainers in front of a mirror. One of them oozes out the words, "Muito agradável."

I pick up a pair of large gray shorts with deep zip pockets and a medium-size black Los Angeles Lakers hoodie. It has the number 6 stitched in gold on it and, underneath, the name James. I head toward the checkout and catch my eye on some navy-blue slippers on the shelf. I get a pair, size eleven.

"You don't have your receipt, love, I can't give you a refund," the pale man says behind the checkout. He looks drained.

"That's bleedin' stupid, isn't it," the young girl yells back.

"Store policy."

"Fuck you and your bleedin' store policy." She storms past me. I just give the pale bloke a sympathizing expression.

"All for two euro," he says to me. I buy the clothing and leg it over to the men's changing room. I peel off the filthy suit, which also has dog hair all over it. My dog, Simone, wouldn't stop jumping on me this morning.

I put the new clothing on. The hoodie is a little tight, but I feel clean. The slippers are comfy. I put my phone, notebook, gloves, and wallet in me pockets. I pop my headphones back into my ears.

I hold the gun in my hand. I see the curtain pull across the changing room I'm in. I look down. The child who was being dragged around earlier by his mother stares at the gun, then me, with his big eyes. I give him a wink and place the gun in my pocket with the silencer.

I get out of there. I don't know which place is worse. Walking among the dead at Mount Jerome Cemetery or shopping in Penneys with all these lunatics.

I get outside and it's raining. Nothing to worry about, just a drizzle, which will soon pass. I dump my old clothing in the bin and rip the price tags off my new clothing. I turn around and see a newsstand between Eason's and Penneys. The seller is buried in newspapers, magazines, and scratch cards. I lean forward to read one of the headlines: "WIFE KILLS HUSBAND."

My phone vibrates in my pocket. I receive a text from the Bronze Man: *Head over to 143 Baggot Street Lower.* I reply with a thumbs-up emoji.

Outside the iconic GPO (General Post Office) building is a bloke wearing a woolly cardigan calmly playing the cello as the Irish flag flaps on top of the building. Beyond the talented cello performer is the 390-foot stainless steel Spire. It looks like a pin. I remove my notebook from my back pocket and cross off my task on my to-do list.

~~PENNEYS~~

CHAPTER THREE

The shooting pain in my shins is still gnawing away at me like a stubborn toothache. I find myself pedaling on D'Olier Street, then onto College Street, passing Trinity College.

The town is still energetic, full of life. Most people are off work on Saturdays and mope about the city like stray dogs. They just want fresh air and to get out of the house.

Not the best day to perform a hit, but when is? I tracked Connor "The Savage" Dunphy for three weeks. I knew his daily routine. Where he went to buy his food, get his hair cut, collect his social welfare payment, his visits to his mate out in Bray, and finally his once-a-week visit to Mount Jerome Cemetery to see his parents' grave. He lived in a busy apartment complex out in Coolock, which would have been too risky a place to get near him.

So, the cemetery was my best option. Funny enough, my mother's grave wasn't too far from his parents', which worked out just perfect. The buildup and performing the hit are the easy part of the job.

It's the disposing of the weapon that I'm always worried about. I could easily wipe the gun down and reuse it, but I don't like to take any chances. Back in 2006, they introduced some hard-hitting penalties for firearm offenses in Ireland. You can get five years' imprisonment for just carrying a gun or ammunition and ten years to life in jail for gun violence.

I'm more paranoid than ever. Maybe having Olivia in my life has changed everything? The thought of not seeing her for one day, let alone years, saddens me deeply.

I was seeing Olivia for months, back when she was an escort, but then things got serious between us when I had to take care of a baby for a week and I paid her to help me with him. I told her I was minding the baby for a friend who was away for a week. She didn't know I'd murdered the baby's father, heard the baby crying, and took him from his crib. The father was a low-life drug dealer, and leaving the baby all alone in that smelly apartment with the corpse didn't feel right. Olivia was hesitant at first to help me out, but she did, and it all worked out in the end.

What was a simple business transaction between me and Olivia has blossomed into something special. Now I'm trying to be extra careful with my actions because from day one since I met her, she thinks I work in a bike shop and not that I kill people for a living.

I glide right on Pembroke Street Lower. Fitzwilliam Square sits quietly to my left, out of the way of the busy streets of the city. Back in the day, the towering Georgian buildings surrounding the square housed residents who entertained between January and St. Patrick's Day. Now the buildings are used as medical, accountancy, and law offices.

I pedal under a very sneaky archway to Quinn's Lane. I press on the back brakes, stopping outside a tall blue gate with a sign that reads **GREGORY'S IRONWORKS**.

I get a fright as I catch a glimpse of my distorted face in the round mirror just above the gate, which is open a few inches. I walk in with my bike. I leave it against the wall and close the gate behind me. There's a red van on the lot with rusty rims and a Liverpool FC logo sticker on the front windscreen.

I hear the static sound of music playing on the radio. A fella breezes out of a steel shed wearing protective gear and giant boots. He lifts up his face shield.

"Paddy," he says to me with a big, hearty smile on his face.

"Gregory," I reply.

"How are we doing on this fine day?" he asks, shaking my hand, still wearing his thick gloves. He's a short man, about five foot three, thin, with a scruffy beard and an asymmetrical mole under his right eyelid that may need seeing to by a dermatologist.

"Grand, just making a little drop-off to the furnace, if that's okay with you?"

"No problem," he says guiding me to his shed. "You want a cup of tea?"

"I'm grand."

"Are you sure? The kettle is already boiled," he says, removing his gloves.

"Go on, then," I reply to be nice. He drops two teabags into two mugs.

"Furnace is all ready for ye," he says with his back to me. I remove the Glock 17 from my pocket, keeping the silencer for another day. I wipe the gun with my shirt and press the button on the machine. It opens up like the mouth of a dragon. I dump the gun in. I press another button. The doors shut. I watch the gun dissolve inside like an ice cream cone melting on a hot day in July.

"What are ye working on this week?" I hand him a hundred euro in cash. He takes it off me, shoving it in his back pocket.

"There's a castle out in Offaly that I'm breaking me back on. They needed these massive Gothic-style gates forged with the family motto and coat of arms… ye want to see?" he asks joyfully.

"Sure."

"Do you take sugar?"

"You don't have any sweeteners?"

"I might do," he says, rummaging through some paper cups filled with packets of sugar. "Found one," he says, eyes wide open as he shakes the pink packet. He stirs a small spoon in the mugs and hands me the milkier tea as we wander outside. "Here she is," he says. Against a tall concrete wall is the gate. It's about twelve feet high, painted black, with the family motto and coat of arms in gold.

"Impressive," I say, sipping on my lukewarm tea. The mug has a smiling unicorn on it.

"Pro Deo et Patria ad Astra," he says.

"What does that mean?"

"Who bleedin' knows." He swallows back half his tea. Some of it starts dripping down his chin.

"It's Latin, meaning, 'For God and Country to the Stars,'" I say, reading the translation off my phone.

"That's mad, isn't it," he says. "Let's hope I spelled it correctly."

"Will that thing fit in the van?"

"It fuckin' better or I'll be charging extra," he says. "The castle is over four hundred years old, can ye believe it?"

"I can't."

"Did you hear about the woman who stabbed her husband?" he asks.

"I saw the headline earlier," I reply.

"Apparently she was being abused by him for years and one day she decides she's had enough," he says. "Stabbed him ten times in the chest." Gregory does a stabbing motion with his hand. "Like something out of a horror movie, blood everywhere, all over the bedsheets and carpet. I feel bad for the kids. They were in the other room when this was all going down."

I shake my head like it's sad news, but it's no surprise. This happens all the time. Women getting abused by their partners is a daily occurrence. Sometimes my job requires me to beat up or threaten an abuser, but then there's that occasion when the woman snaps, sees red, and ends up doing my job.

Killing is a messy business.

It's my cue to leave. If I stay any longer I'll be here all day yapping to Gregory.

"I better be off now." I hand him the empty mug. I roll my bike out of the lot.

"You be careful out there," he shouts. "People are losing the plot."

~~GREGORY'S IRONWORKS~~

CHAPTER FOUR

Every year, many Dubliners and visitors from around the world will attempt the "Baggot Mile." It consists of drinking in twelve pubs on one street. Well, at least attempting to. When you have nearly eight hundred pubs in Dublin alone, which is similar in size to Walt Disney World Resort and the Bronx, people are going to have fun with it.

Pubs are almost next door to each other or on every corner. This pub crawl is not for the fainthearted and most will fail miserably, and rightly so. Most will be plastered, cockeyed, and slurring their words by pub number five or six.

The paths are damp and the bumpy roads look greasy. The sun bounces off the slated rooftops, blinding my precious eyes. My stomach continues to rumble and make strange noises I haven't heard before as I cycle. Hour sixteen into the fast. I'm starting to feel it now as I make my way past a burrito bar. I pinch my belly, which feels like I'm wearing one of those fake pregnancy stomachs made out of silicone.

I get off my bike and lock it tightly outside a busy café with flashy orange chairs. On the corner is one of Ireland's oldest pubs, Toners. Established in 1734, painted red and black, and one to tick off your list on the Baggot Mile.

Across the road is a Tesco Express, and above it is a gym. I watch a young man's face turn purple as he performs a squat. My gut tells me he might pass out on the next rep. I continue walking. A nice breeze blows against the hairs on my legs and my gunslinger mustache.

The clothing on my back feels too new and needs to be thrown in the wash. God only knows who was touching the clothes before I bought them.

A bloke with a cigarette sticking out between his dry lips is on a ladder. The ash falls to the ground, then blows away. I tilt my neck back, glancing at him as he secures the sign hanging from two chains, a snow-white owl with yellow eyes. Across the entrance in black lettering it reads **THE CRAZY OWL**.

I go inside. A waitress wearing a three-piece suit is setting the tables. At the bar are red-cushioned stools and on the countertop are Victorian beaded table lamps in blues and gold, with copper fringes. The wallpaper has a rose pattern, matching the carpet. The bar is low lit and the red-and-white stripy ceiling is entrancing.

My boss, the Bronze Man, is standing on a stage. She got this name because of her countless visits to Portugal. Her precious skin has gone from a pasty white to a very tanned color, almost bronze-looking. She took over the hit agency when her father was murdered a few years ago.

In my twenties, I spent my days scrubbing toilets and floors in a chipper. That's when I met the Bronze Man and her father. They ran a quaint pub and were looking for a security doorman. I didn't have an ounce of fat on me from all the pills I was popping, but they took me in, and I haven't looked back since. She can be ruthless and a real pain in the arse. She's like the sister I never had.

"I feel like I'm inside a bloody circus," I say to the Bronze Man.

She steps off the stage wearing a tailored dark brown suit, white turtleneck, and brown Oxford platform shoes. She gives me a firm handshake. Her nails are cut short, coated with the color raspberry.

"Honest truth, what do you think of the place?" She fires the question at me. Her tan is fading away, but her hair is still red like the fur on a Dublin fox.

"It's very… you," I reply, taking another glance at the place.

She makes a fist. "You mean ambitious, chic, sophisticated, and full of spunk."

"Exactly. Not sure I'm dressed the part, though."

"We'll need to fix that," she says.

Slim the Bodyguard steps out from the hallway with his long, lush hair pushed behind his ears. He has the usual serious facial expression and cutthroat demeanor.

He nods at me and says, "Patrick."

"Slim," I reply. He brushes past me. A man of very few words. He quietly sits at the bar. His coat drapes over the stool like a cape.

"Drinks and live jazz music, sounds exciting," I say as we stand in front of the stage. A dark fella with flawless skin has his white sleeves rolled up and starts playing the piano with care and professionalism, like a young Thelonious Monk. On the side of the bulky piano it reads **BÖSENDORFER** in fancy gold lettering. I take a peek inside the piano. "This thing is big enough to hide a body," I say. The man on the piano gives me a puzzled expression as he continues to play.

To the right of the stage, dressed the same, is a stocky-built chap with a goatee on the double bass.

"How did everything go with Connor Dunphy?" she asks.

"It went well."

"Let's talk in the back," she says. "Lads, I need something more up-tempo." She raises her voice, snapping her fingers. "This is opening night. I want people to be having a good time, not to fall asleep."

I follow her through a narrow hallway. The wallpaper is the color of poached salmon. We pass the restrooms, then come to a dead end.

"Where the hell are you taking me?" In front of us on the wall is a painting in an antique silver frame. "What's the name of this one?"

"*The Red Rose* by John Lavery," she says. "This is his wife, Lady Hazel Lavery." The woman in the painting has milky skin and sits relaxed in an elegant golden chair wearing a purple dress, delicately holding a rose to her neck, daydreaming. Behind her are red drapes. The Bronze Man pushes the wall with her hand and like a door it opens wide.

"Sneaky," I whisper.

"Welcome to my speakeasy," she says. Inside the room it's dark, with very few light fixtures hanging from the ceiling. The bar to the left is small but has at least a hundred bottles of hard liquor.

Dark shelves are filled with antique leather books. It looks like a library belonging to Trinity College. This is heaven. Drinking and reading, what else could you ask for.

There's something magical about the place, something secretive. Imagine chatting with famous dead people about books and art while sipping on whiskey or wine. I wonder what Oscar Wilde drank.

"Take a seat," she says.

We sit down in a red velvet booth. It's comfy. A thick-wristed woman in her thirties places two drink menus on the table. She's wearing a leather apron like a butcher. She has tattoos on her forearms, but not of flowers or angels. On the inside of her forearm is a woman with an octopus head lifting up her skirt.

The Bronze Man says, "This is my cousin, Caitríona," which is pronounced *Ka-TREE-na*. Most people who live outside Ireland will slaughter the name. I nod to the broad-shouldered woman. She's built like a buffalo, with a mullet hairstyle. I open up the menu. A white envelope is inside.

"Payment," the Bronze Man says. "I hope the hit didn't cause you any trouble?"

"I would have preferred to kill him at his flat, but he lived in a busy apartment complex."

"I'm down to three hit men on the books," she says, reading the menu.

"What happened to the others?"

"Brian in Galway has retired. He wants to spend his days fishing and hiking. Brian was always a strange fellow."

"He's only forty years of age," I say. Caitríona comes back to the table with a bowl of peanuts. I get a look at the tattoo on her other forearm. It's a massive grasshopper.

I feel so empty inside. If I did vomit, it would be nothing but air. I notice a long hair sprouting from Caitríona's chin. I get a closer look at her face. She isn't wearing makeup and has thick eyebrows like Colin Farrell, which I couldn't take my eyes off.

"Harry in Limerick moved to the States. He met someone," Caitríona says.

"What's her name?" I ask. I can smell the salt on the nuts.

"Andrew."

"I didn't know he was…you know." Caitríona snaps the menu out of my hands.

"That's 'cause you're oblivious," the Bronze Man says. My body feels cold. I glance at the time on my phone. "Are you okay?" she asks, pointing at one of the drinks on the menu. She makes a two-finger gesture to Caitríona, who then goes back to the bar.

"I'm fasting," I say.

"I should really do that, ye know. I've only heard good things," she says, picking up a peanut and slipping it in her gob, licking the salt off her fingertips. "It's good for weight loss, brain function—"

"You said you only have three hit men on the books. Me, the Cork fella, and Timmy."

"Timmy is dead."

"Dead? How did that happen?"

"Heart attack."

"Jesus," I say.

"Loved the white powder a bit too much."

"Then who's the third?"

"Eagle Eye is back in the game." I have no response. "I know you two have fallen out recently, but we have work to be done. I even sold the villa in the Algarve to buy this place."

"I was just about to ask you about your villa."

"I've had my last trip to Portugal for a while, unfortunately," she says. "Didn't you go away somewhere, Greece... or was it... Croatia, that's it, Croatia. Lovely country."

"Montenegro," I say. "I went to Montenegro."

"I reckon that cost ye a pretty penny?"

"Yes, but Olivia was adamant we go half."

"Oh, that was very nice of her. I'm sure she's made a decent living from her escorting days."

"All I can say is that the trip was pleasant and headache-free."

"Are you insinuating I give you headaches?" she asks.

"I would never say such a thing to my boss."

"I need a glass of water," she says. "Those bloody nuts. Caitríona here is in charge of all the jobs. I'll divide the workload between you and Eagle Eye for now, is that okay?"

"If he doesn't get in my way, we'll be fine."

"I have too much to deal with at the moment," she says.

Caitríona comes walking over with two cocktails and two waters on a tray. She places everything neatly on the table.

"I'll be in contact with you soon for your next job," Caitríona says. "Give us your phone." Her voice is deep, harsh, and unforgiving. She snatches the phone out of my hand and starts typing with her thumbs. "This is my number," she says, throwing the phone on my lap. "I don't fuck around, if I text or call you at any time, you respond, hear me?"

"Yes, Jesus," I say. The Bronze Man gently smirks.

"Cheers," she says as we click our drinks.

"What is this?" I ask. I take another sip.

"It's called a sidecar."

"Really?" I look at the time. Twelve o'clock. It's feeding time. I can finally eat. I reach for the bowl of nuts and feel nothing. It's empty. "For fuck's sake, you're a savage," I say to the Bronze Man, standing up. I lash the rest of the cocktail back. "I need real food. Talk to ye soon."

"I'll be in touch," says Caitríona, arms folded. The grasshopper tattoo on her forearm gazes at me with bulbous eyes as I exit the speakeasy.

"You should bring Olivia to the bar," the Bronze Man yells through both hands. I stick up my middle finger at her.

BAGGOT STREET

CHAPTER FIVE

I cycle for eight minutes. I'm starving. I lock my bike outside St. Werburgh's Church of Ireland on Werburgh Street. Next to the entrance of the church is a circular plaque that reads:

> **JOHN FIELD**
> **COMPOSER AND PIANIST**
> **BORN AT GOLDEN LANE**
> **26-7-1782**
> **DIED AT MOSCOW 27-1-1837**
> **CREATOR OF THE NOCTURNE**
> **PRECURSOR OF CHOPIN**
> **WAS BAPTIZED IN THIS CHURCH**
> **5-9-1782**

How very interesting. I quickly turn around and find what I'm looking for. **LEO BURDOCKS, FAMOUS FISH AND CHIPS SINCE 1913.** Dublin's oldest chipper. I can smell the crispy batter on the cod and the freshly cut potato chips in the fryer. My stomach is growling like a grass frog.

I step inside and place an order. I have no time for small talk. The workers behind the counter are all wearing white coats like they are about to perform surgery. A young man peeling potatoes with a knife is sweating in the corner.

I wait patiently for the fish to be fried. I check inside the envelope that was handed to me earlier. Six grand cash in total for killing a man who slaughtered his wife. A good day at the office. Though it's always a nice feeling to get paid, it's also good to have another scumbag off the streets. Fair is fair. The bastard deserved to die. Now, that might not be a pleasant thing to say out loud, but I do believe some people don't deserve a second chance. Connor Dunphy was a little rat that needed to be exterminated.

I have to be even more careful with my kills this time around, while fasting. I'm only on day one and my body will need to adapt. The Bronze Man was right about fasting improving brain function. The cemetery hit was smooth and silky for sure. I felt sharper, on my toes. It wasn't until after the hit that I was somewhat agitated, light-headed, knowing I needed to eat.

The bloke drenches the chips in salt and vinegar. I can't wait to get my hands on them. Behind him is a glass case displaying the names of a bunch of celebrities who have eaten at the chipper, including Metallica, Liam Neeson, Russell Crowe, Charlize Theron, Ron Howard, Bruce Springsteen, the cast of *P.S. I Love You*, and Jackie Chan. There are way more names on the wall, but I can't be bothered reading them all.

"Enjoy," the old fella says with his thick, dirty mustache covering his lips. He hands me the fish and chip wrapped in white paper. It's incredibly hot. I sit back down and open it up like it's a Christmas gift, but way better. The heat hits my face. I bite into one chip. It's soft, but I have to spit it out, it's that hot. I start blowing on the chips. I'm going to need a bleedin' fan to cool these things down.

My fingers are all salty. It starts stinging my middle finger where I cut my nail too short. I can detect the scent of pungent vinegar on the chips. I remember when I was a boy I used to see mothers spray vinegar and water on their windows to clean them.

I haven't had this meal in a long time. Working as a cleaner in a chipper back in the day put me off wanting to eat it ever again. This time it's different. I'm hungry and this is the best chipper in town.

I stick my headphones in my ears and play "Sweet Leaf" by Black Sabbath. Bill Ward and Geezer Butler nearly blow up my eardrums and I turn the volume down. Swallowing back my food like a horse, I quickly feel my stomach expand.

I'm so full already I can only eat half the battered fish, which is bigger than my head. After a dozen or so chips, I'm done for. My belly is bursting and my gums have salt and vinegar rubbed all over them. I wrap everything back up and bring it with me under my arm. I use the hand sanitizer at the entrance. I grab a bottle of water on the way out and swallow it all back, losing my breath.

I get back on my bike and slowly make my way home. Crowds of people linger about in Temple Bar and on the quays. I arrive in Smithfield Square. Traditional music is playing and I'm sure it will continue late into the evening.

I push my bike into the lobby. Nicholas, the young bloke who works at the front desk, waves at me.

"Those packages came about an hour ago," he says, removing his headphones. He disappears into the back room. "Here ye go," he says, handing me a small box and a cardboard envelope. "Your partner had a few deliveries come by earlier in a big truck."

"Did she?"

"A few big ones."

"Interesting. How's *The Lord of the Rings* going?" I ask him.

"The font in the book was too small, so I switched to the audiobook, which feels like I'm listening to a bleedin' musical at times," he says.

"Tolkien was a poet, after all," I say, wheeling my bike into the elevator, packages in hand.

"Was he? I didn't know that," he says.

"Let me know how the rest of the book goes."

"I'll have my verdict soon," he yells as the elevator doors shut.

I open the apartment door with the leftover food in one hand and the packages in the other. I push the bike inside.

Simone comes running over to me eagerly, wagging her long tail. Loud music of some sort is playing and a whiff of jasmine is in the air. I leave my bike by the door.

"What is that?" I shout over the music being played on the TV. I put my packages on the floor.

"Ngoni," Olivia yells back, adjusting the couch as her full, luscious afro shakes.

"Can you turn it down?"

"What?"

I grab the remote from the coffee table and mute the TV, my jaw tightening in frustration. "Jesus, what is that?" I ask her, staring at the TV, which shows an African fella wearing all blue sitting down playing a stringed instrument in what seems to be the African wing of a museum.

"It's traditional Mali music. They use this guitar instrument made of calabash and dried animal skin head," she says, face beaming with tiredness.

"Jaysus." I'm confused, feeling like I'm in a different continent.

"What do ye think?" she asks. I offer her a nervous smile. "I knew you would like it." I put my food on the kitchen island. I empty my pockets and leave my things on the counter. Simone is scratching at my leg, sulking at me with her big Labrador eyes.

"What's that smell?" Olivia opens up the paper. "Fish and chips! I thought you were going to eat healthy this week."

"It's for the dog. I only had a few nibbles."

"Don't give her the fish—there might be bones in it," she says, a little peeved. I have a chip in my hand. The dog sees it and trots in a circle like one of those horses in a dressage event. She reaches for the chip and snags it from my fingertips. She chews on it ferociously. I pour the rest of chips into her dog bowl, removing the sharp ones.

"Here ye go." I rub her head.

"And no more junk food for you," Olivia says, looking at me, then at the dog. "Or you, missy." I wash the salt and vinegar from my hands with soap in the kitchen sink. I hear Simone scoffing the chips down. "Now, just take it all in before you say anything," Olivia says, grabbing my arm, not giving me chance to dry my hands or breathe. "This here on the wall above the TV is a Marka."

"What's a Marka?"

"A tribal mask used in ceremonies to ensure a successful hunt," she replies with her arms folded. "And I think they wear it during circumcision ceremonies."

"You think?"

"I know, I know, you must think it's stupid. I was born in Cork and my dad was from Mali but I'm just trying to get in touch with my African roots. After all I'm half-African." I scratch my head. "Is it a bit too excessive?"

"No, it's just... different. I've never seen anything like this before except in museums or on the History Channel." The dog looks sluggish after the chips.

I glance around the living room. There are plenty of green plants, a colorful tribal rug under the coffee table, decorative pillow cushions with red African women printed on them, and a hunched-over terra-cotta figure in a spinal-twist pose beside the TV. Olivia also has burning incense sticks on the side table with a baby cactus.

I suppose my books are neatly lined up on shelves on the walls. She hasn't completely left me out. I squint my face.

"What's wrong?" she asks.

"My shins are killing me."

"Sit down, you need to relax." I lie down on the couch and take a deep breath. I put my feet up on the round ottoman she drags over. She runs off to the fridge. "This should help." She places a bag of frozen peas on top of my legs. "You should see a doctor."

"I'll see one next week."

"What happened to your suit?"

"I binned it."

"What do you mean you binned it?"

"It was a cheap suit, and you know I never like wearing those things."

"You should have kept it. You never know when you will need a black suit again. Isn't your boss on his last legs?"

"Who? Jack? He's just old, but he's not dying."

"Did you buy flowers for your mother's grave?" she asks. Her demeanor sounds like she's ready for an argument, which is surprising considering we just came back from a lovely holiday in Montenegro and moved in together.

"Yes, I did," I reply, glaring up at her. She stares back at me like something is wrong. Like she knew I put three bullets in Connor "The Savage" Dunphy's chest and two in his head. "So, what's the plan of action? Do you know what kind of work you want to do since your escorting days are behind you?"

"I haven't a clue." She takes a deep breath. "I'm going to take a shower. I'm exhausted."

My phone vibrates on the kitchen countertop. "Here," she says, handing me my phone. Olivia starts walking up the stairs.

"What? No kiss?"

"I'm all sticky," she shouts back.

"I might join you in that shower," I yell out. I look down at my phone and my stomach starts fluttering and my chest tightens. The name "Nocturnal" pops up on the screen. The message reads: *Meet me at my place tomorrow morning.*

Nocturnal was Olivia's sadistic pimp. I offered him a lot of money so she wouldn't have to work for him anymore, but I came up short on payment. So, I did a heist for him and we came to an agreement that I would do a couple of jobs for him in the future. I have a sickly feeling my time has come.

The worst part is lying to Olivia about all this. She thinks I did a simple drop for Nocturnal in return for him letting her out of his escort service and that we're both done with him. I really hope she didn't see his name pop up on my phone. I quickly look around the room. I glance up at the shelf and see the name Ray Bradbury. I change the contact name in my phone from Nocturnal to Ray.

The dog jumps up on the couch and makes herself comfortable on my legs. "Simone, relax, will ye." She starts licking her paws. I can feel her tongue graze my knee.

I rip open one of the packages. Inside is a Nikon D3500 camera. My eyes are too drowsy to be squinting into the eyepiece. I open the cardboard envelope and remove a small book, *The Servant of Two Masters* by Italian playwright Carlo Goldoni. I haven't read any of his works yet, but I'm looking forward to it. I put them aside and tilt my head back. I hear my neck lightly crack like a pencil.

I stare at the narrow iron mask mounted on the wall. It has paper-thin eyes and mouth, an elongated nose, and antelope antlers. Terrifying-looking thing. The bag of frozen peas falls off my shins and onto the floor. Simone lets out a wet sneeze. My eyelids slowly start to close. I can faintly hear the shower running upstairs and Olivia calling out my name.

CHAPTER SIX

The next morning. My eyes open up to the frightening mask on the wall. I'm still on the couch, with a blanket over me. Simone is lying on my back. I look at the time on my phone: nine o'clock. This must be one of the longest sleeps I've ever had in my life.

My body aches as I stand up. The dog jumps off the couch, limping over to her bowl of water. She has dead legs. I know the feeling too well. I do some stretches, letting out a yawn. I fill the kettle up with water and turn it on. I pour myself a glass of water and swallow it back quickly. I can hear it go down my throat.

I walk up the stairs and see Olivia sleeping. She looks peaceful, and the temptation to slide in the bed and spoon her feels nice and warm, but I resist. I strip down and jump into the shower.

The bathroom has a strong odor of bleach. I spent hours cleaning the new loft a few nights ago. I was on toilet duty, scrubbing the tiles, sink, mirror, and shower door. I jump out of the shower and dry myself. The room fills with steam. I open the door slightly and wipe the mirror above the sink.

I lather myself up with body lotion and use unscented deodorant under my arms. I brush my teeth, spitting into the sink. I taste blood in my mouth. I've brushed too hard. I floss and use mouthwash. That feels better.

The fan above my head is annoyingly loud. The room is in desperate need of a small window for some delicious fresh air.

I quietly put on some clean clothes, dumping the new ones I bought yesterday in the wash basket, except for the Lakers hoodie, which smells okay. I tie my long wet silver hair into a ponytail.

The bedroom overlooks the spacious living room and kitchen area. It has a classic New York feel to it, with exposed red brick and grand windows that ooze out sunlight like a church. The ceilings are fifteen feet high with wooden panels painted white. The rent is five hundred euro cheaper and the place is bigger than the last place I lived in near the Grand Canal.

The price of rent keeps going up in Dublin, pissing off everybody in the country. The problem is that it's expensive everywhere in the world today unless you want to live in feckin' Bangkok.

I walk down to the kitchen and make myself a cup of tea. The next time I can eat is not for another two hours and I've really messed up my sleep schedule. I open the balcony door and a cool breeze blows on my naked legs. I go outside and lean over the balcony. It's no Central Park, but it's a quaint little square with character and charisma offering up hip coffee shops, bistros, a cinema, a trendy hostel, a food market, and a peculiar giant checkered teapot sculpture.

Across the way is one of Ireland's tallest landmarks, the Chimney Viewing Tower, built in 1895 and originally used to distill Jameson whiskey. Now it's a tourist hot spot for Jameson whiskey tasting and dining. The proper distillery is down in Cork.

I look across the way to the other building and see a woman sitting up in bed. The partner enters the room, hands her a glass of orange juice, kisses her on the cheek.

I finish my tea and go back inside, putting on my slippers. "Want to go for a walk?" I whisper to Simone. Her tail sways left to right like a windscreen wiper. I attach the leash to her collar and we go to the elevator.

The lobby is dead. An old curly-haired woman is at the front desk this morning. She gazes at me as she sips on her mug of coffee, which I can smell from a mile away. I get outside and the frail sunlight emerges from the transparent clouds. I have the urge to sneeze but I manage to hold it in. I plop my John Lennon–like sunglasses on and browse across the square.

Simone is already urinating by a tree. We do a lap around the square, watching a few morning joggers fly by us, sweating and breathing heavily. The dog lets out a high-pitched bark and nearly yanks my arm out of the socket as I grip the leash. Yesterday this place was packed with people drinking, dancing, and singing. Now it's dead. A typical Sunday.

We head back to the loft. I close the door behind me and let the dog off the leash. There's a strong odor of smoke inside. The balcony door is open wide. Oliva is outside. When I get closer, I see her smoking a cigarette, which is strange since she gave them up months ago. She turns her head and sees me holding the leash in my hand. She's in her pajamas as she puts out her cigarette in a flowerpot. The last of the smoke blows out from the side of her mouth and spews from her nostrils.

"Morning," I say to her. She has her arms folded and a displeased expression splashed across her face. She gets closer to me. I can smell the cigarette off her.

"Explain what this is," she says, lobbing the thick envelope full of cash to me. I catch it in my hands. It's hard to explain, since we've only been together for a few months, and I've been telling her I work at a bike shop.

"Jack owed me some money. I gave him a loan months ago for bike parts."

"I don't believe ye! Tell me the truth—are you working with Nocturnal?" The name haunts the room like a ghost. "You said to me that you only did one favor for him, and that was it!"

"And I did, I swear to God," I say to her, acting the dummy with my hands up like she's pointing a gun at me. "I'm done with him—I told you this already."

"Then why all the cash?"

The dog starts moaning. She can tell we're fighting. She scratches my shin, peeling the skin off a little.

"Jack is an old fella, he does everything in cash," I say. "I haven't seen him ever use cards. He says to me all the time, 'I don't trust those poxy banks.'"

Olivia stares deep into my eyes as she listens to my response like I'm in a confession box. She shakes her head, and a smile slowly appears on her face. I've passed the test, what a relief. I walk over to her, giving her a hug.

"Promise me you're telling me the truth," she says. "I don't want to lose you."

"I promise." I edge closer to her. "You know... you should really give up smoking."

"I know, I know."

"I should go deposit this money at the bank, okay?" I say, leaning in, kissing her soft lips tasting of nicotine. She's so beautiful as the sunlight enters the loft. At five feet nine inches with smooth light-brown skin, she's a stunner. She strokes my beard with her fingers, fanning out my mustache.

"This needs a trim," she says.

"Tell me all about it. I'll be back before you know it."

"Maybe I should start looking for work on Monday. Being cooped up in this loft is driving me mad." She looks out the balcony window. "It's a lovely day. We should go for a walk around Grafton Street."

"Sounds like a good plan."

"We'll do it when you get back. I can wear my new shirt I bought the other day." The dog continues to moan by our feet.

"She's getting jealous," I say. I gaze into her eyes. "You know I love you."

"I love you too."

CHAPTER SEVEN

I fill Simone's bowls up with food and fresh water. I then leave the loft with my bike. I start cycling, making my way on the quays.

It wasn't too long ago that Olivia and I spent a month in Montenegro soaking up the sun like two seals on the 117 beaches they had to offer, except for the rocky ones, of course. Nobody wants to walk on a stony beach—are you out of your mind? No, you want to lie down on a sunbed, sizzle for an hour, and end up sunburned under a palm tree, unable to move.

We stayed in a private villa with a pool in the charming countryside, then an eighteenth-century baroque stone boutique hotel overlooking the Bay of Kotor, followed by a tiny yacht on the port of Bijela, and one night we just sprawled out on a beach, bellies full, under the stars. We even brought the dog along.

We ate delicious food, drank exotic cocktails, and made deep, passionate love, which on the one hand was incredible, but on the other, tiring. On one occasion I nearly pulled my back.

Luckily, I didn't have to pay Olivia's half of the trip. I'm not a rich man. I wear cheap clothing, I have no car or children, and I try to get my hair cut every couple of months. My big expenses are the rent on the loft and buying guns.

The trip was blissful, but after two weeks you just want to go back home, back to the filthy streets of Dublin, pondering, staring at the ominous clouds full of threatening rain.

I arrive on my bike from Smithfield to Leeson Street. I lock my bike across the road. Two men are carefully painting sash windows on the Cyprus embassy. The country's flag is simplistic, with the shape of the island in copper-orange and two olive branches underneath. The background is white. The European flag is also fluttering in the wind beside it, almost touching it. No days off for the painters, not even on a Sunday.

The conditions today are almost perfect, gray and windy. With my backpack on, I head over to the attractive Georgian building with the black door. The door knocker is the head of a majestic lion, solid, cast from iron like the one on 10 Downing Street. I knock hard, twice. It's loud, making a dense sound, which I'm sure most people would have heard on the street.

The heavy door opens up. A big man wearing a baggy black suit looks down at me with a disgusting expression on his round Eastern European face, as if he's going to utter the words *Who the fuck are you?*

"I'm here to see N—"

He nods before I can say the rest of his name. He gestures again to get inside. I walk in. It's been a good few months since I've been here. I was hoping to never come back to this hellhole.

It still has the red carpet on the old wooden floorboards, the softly lit gold chandeliers hanging from the ceilings, and the fruity smells of perfumes that could make your head melt lingering in the hallway. But today I'm getting the hint of spice, pepper and cinnamon.

The big man's stomach almost touches me. He turns and walks ahead and I follow him. We walk past the red walls and the red throne with a gold frame casually sitting at the end of the hallway.

I take a sneak peek into the dark room to my right. There's a half-naked fella on his knees wearing a leather gimp mask, a rubber ball lodged in his mouth. His hands are cuffed behind his back and he has a collar on like a dog. The man is shiny, looking slippery, whimpering through the mask.

A woman in a tight, glossy black dress made from plastic materials is standing behind the poor fella on his knees. She has a brownish cowboy hat on and is swinging a long silver chain like she's at a rodeo event in Texas.

Her eyes are coated in purple eye shadow with glued-on fluttering fake eyelashes, and her lips are painted black. Her white-powdered face glows in the dark room as she locks the chain on his neck collar. She pulls on him mercilessly, gritting her vampire-like teeth. His hairy bare chest stretches as she yanks on the chain. He releases a long groan.

We keep moving. The big fella the size of a bull opens a door. I go inside. The living space is huge, similar to a dance hall. I remember it vividly. The last time I was in this room, I was tied upside down with my hands bound. It took weeks for my shoulder to recover when I fell to the floor.

"Patrick," says a voice in a posh English accent. I look around in the dark. "How is one of my favorite acquaintances doing today?" I move closer. There's a tall lamp shining near Nocturnal. He's sitting up straight at a narrow wooden table about twelve feet in length. The room is opaque, with hints of light seeping through the cracks of the closed curtains, and it's cool, like I'm standing in the frozen-food aisle at a supermarket.

He's wearing a classic gray checked sports jacket, single-breasted with shawl lapels. Underneath is a white silk shirt and a navy-blue cravat with white dots like the one Clark Gable wore in that film *Gone with the Wind*, minus the hair and ridiculous tan.

"I'm doing well," I reply.

"And how was your trip to Montenegro? I haven't been myself, but I've only heard good things."

"Are you spying on me?"

He turns his head toward the dim light coming from the lamp, which shows his perfectly bald head and his skin the color of a white dolphin. "I have my eyes and ears about."

A little person dressed like the head butler from *Downtown Abbey* comes marching in with a classic serving tray, aluminum, gently placed on his tiny fingers.

He dramatically flicks a cloth dinner napkin like you see at fancy restaurants with his other hand and places it on Nocturnal's lap. I can see the top of the little fella's head sneaking above the table. He lifts up the dome cover and lays the plate of food on the table, sliding it toward Nocturnal. "Fetch my guest a chair," he says to the little fella.

I sit across the table.

"Vegan steak," he states, cutting into the lump of cement on his plate. "I'm trying out something new."

There aren't any vegetables or sauce to go with it. It looks miserable. I wouldn't even feed my dog the thing.

"Delightful," I say.

"You want some? I can get my chef to whip you up a meal. He can cook anything."

"I'm fasting."

"Oh, how exciting." Nocturnal cuts a small piece of his meal and lodges it in his mouth, swallowing hard. It looks sore going down his pipe.

"What's the verdict?"

"Vile," he replies, dabbing his mouth with a napkin. "But one must eat."

I wish I had a gun on me right now. I could put one in his bald head then two in the big man behind me and finally in the little fella. But this is too risky. If it all went haywire, Olivia and I would have to run away. It makes me queasy thinking about it.

"What kind of job do you want me to do?"

"It's pretty straightforward. A man of your reputation shouldn't have any troubles with this one," he says, pushing the plate to the side. "I need you to do a pickup." He removes a folded piece of paper from his trouser pocket and slides it to me across the table. I reach my hand out, pick it up, and open it like he handed me a birthday card.

"Ruby Collins, Airfield Estate," I read out loud.

"I need you to bring him to me sedated, in one piece."

"Sedated, what do you mean sedated?"

"I want you to use this," he says, standing up, the chair scraping, searching through his suit jacket. He pulls something out and holds it up to the light. I squint my eyes.

"What's that?"

"A tranquilizer dart," he replies, pinching what looks like a syringe with a bushy pink feather on the end of it. "It's all ready to go, so be very careful. You don't want to be on the other end of this."

I stand up. "So, you want me to sedate this Ruby Collins with this thing." I cautiously remove the dart from his lean fingers. I stare intensely at it. I've never used such a thing in my life.

"Yes, and I want you to bring him unharmed to the Mansion House at six o'clock sharp this evening."

"This evening? Where's the gun to shoot the dart?"

"I don't have the time to be buying dart guns, Mr. Callen."

"How do I get him to the Mansion House? I don't drive."

"I'm sure you'll figure it out, you're a smart cat." He smiles, eyes steely blue.

"You should have told me to do this sooner, like yesterday or the day before," I say. "So I have time to organize myself."

"What's the fun in that?"

I start to go, but before I am out the door, he says, "Tell Olivia I said hi. I do sure miss her around here."

CHAPTER EIGHT

Tonight, I have to kidnap some poor fucker called Ruby Collins and escort him to the Mansion House located on Dawson Street. And I'm there thinking it's going to be a calm Sunday.

My eyeballs sting like crazy when I step outside. The big fella slams the door behind me.

There're piles of construction going on near St. Stephen's Green, so I decide to pedal through the park from the Leeson Street entrance.

The tender sculpture *Three Fates* welcomes me. The three women are robed and hooded, each holding a piece of thread. In Nordic mythology, the Three Fates, known as Norns, lived beside the Well of Urðr. They would water the roots of Yggdrasil, a sacred tree, to keep it from drying out.

I continue cycling on the wet paths, which I'm probably not allowed to do, dodging a few people holding on to their sandwiches in crinkled tinfoil. I get a whiff of pizza, and now I'm hungry, craving something warm and doughy in my mouth.

I check my phone. It's a little after twelve. This fasting is really driving me into insanity and it's only been a couple of days.

I pass the head of James Joyce behaving all somber, judging me through his pince-nez-style spectacles. I'm sure he didn't get a good look at my face. He was known to have poor eyesight. I remember reading in the paper that a pair of his glasses sold for seventeen thousand euro, utter madness.

The park is chockful of rich lime trees, exquisite evergreen oak, birch, holly, hawthorn, laurel, and weeping ash.

I escape west of the park, passing the splendid bronze statue of a gazing Arthur Edward Guinness, reclining in his classic chair facing the Royal College of Surgeons. His mustache is similar to mine, but less offensive. The groundskeepers are on their knees, working hard, planting lavender flowers around him.

I sneak my way across the tram tracks. The bike seat lets out a squeaking sound and I end up on York Street. The Swan Bar is on the corner. Cozy little spot with all types of goers facing the flats and a dry cleaner with horrible graffiti. I swing a smooth right into the narrow bike lane on Aungier Street.

A minute later I'm outside a café called the Bald Barista. The sign above the door is bright orange and features a wrinkly old fella with a bald head. I lock my bike on a rack next to the café and I am already smelling coffee and pastries when I enter.

I order a cup of Irish tea with one milk and one sugar. I press my finger on the glass food display case and ask the woman, "What are those things?" She has coal-black hair with a lightning-gray streak falling to the side of her face.

"Homemade energy balls," she says. "They're gluten-free and vegan-friendly." Her enthusiasm has persuaded me.

"Go on, then, give us two, please."

I also order a toasted cheese sandwich. I see fresh cakes behind the glass, which I would love to get my hands on.

"Is that all?" she asks, waiting patiently for my response.

Everything smells so good. I lean forward, almost pressing my face against the glass. I point at a slice of rich banana bread with walnuts.

"Just the one slice. That will be all."

I need to get in all my meals before the job this evening. The grilled cheese is hot and gooey when it arrives at my table. On the side of the plate are a handful of cheese-and-onion crisps. My breath is going to be ghastly by the time I finish. I get more milk for my tea and eat the rest of my sandwich.

The banana bread is so satisfying. However, the vegan balls are rotten little things that taste dry in my mouth. I leg it out of the café with a full belly and crisps stuck between my teeth. I have to fit in another two big meals before my fast begins again.

Sedating Ruby Collins and hauling his arse back into town will take at least two hours to achieve if all goes well. I will need a couple of things to make this go as smooth as possible. I remove my notebook and starting making a list.

Olivia is going to flip out. She already suspected something was up when she found the envelope filled with cash, and now this.

I call her on my phone. My knee is shaking as I sit on my bike waiting for her to answer. I bite down hard on the nail of my middle finger.

"Hello," Olivia says. "Are you on your way?"

"I have to go into work, love," I say. "Jack isn't feeling too well."

"But you said you were only going to the bank... What about our plans?" she says, furious.

"I know, but work needs me."

"Oh, so you need to fix bikes on a bloody Sunday? When are we going to spend time together?"

"Didn't we just come back from a holiday?"

"That was different. It's the same argument with you, I'm sick of it!"

"How else am I going to pay the bills? It's just me and Jack working at the shop. He needs me."

"No, I need you. It doesn't matter anyways. You're going to do what you want." She hangs up.

Fuck! Fuck! Fuck!

TO-DO LIST

JACK MAGEE

GUN

RUBY COLLINS

THE MANSION HOUSE

CHAPTER NINE

I have no choice but to take this job. If I don't, Nocturnal might hurt Olivia. That was the deal.

I get off Aungier Street, which is starting to get rowdy. I turn right on Camden Row, then left on Heytesbury Street, where it's nice and still, almost slow motion, away from all the hustle and bustle. Any moment now, the ghost of Luciano Pavarotti is going to jump out and start singing "Ave Maria."

Pleasants Street. I roll up on my bike, lifting my right leg up the air like I'm performing a ballet pose. I wheel my bike closer to a building that resembles an old fire station. I see a sign on the front door: **SORRY, WE'RE CLOSED, BE BACK SOON!** I push on the door. It's locked. He usually leaves it open, the bastard.

"Hello!" I yell out. "Jack, are ye in?" I thump my fist on the door, rattling the glass.

"Patrick," I hear my name echo, but where? I step back and look around, my head bobbing like a feckin' pigeon's. "Up here, ye bleedin' imbecile." I look up, and lo and behold, Jack is staring down at me from on top of the bleedin' roof. I can see his big, bushy beard, all white and wild.

"What are ye doing up there?"

"Come up and I'll show you," he replies, letting out a hearty cackle. "Come around the side and climb up the ladder." Jesus Christ. I lock my bike up around a pole with a **NO RIGHT TURN** sign attached to it. I start climbing the flimsy ladder on the side of the redbrick building. It's two stories high. Enough to break both legs or your neck if you were to accidentally fall.

I reach the top of the roof. My hands are now wet from the rails. Jack is standing a few feet away from me with a bloody bow and arrow in his hands.

"Are you all right in the head?" I ask him, catching my breath.

"Look at this... Isn't she magnificent?" He lifts the bow up in front of him. I've never seen him this giddy before. "Oak Ridge Bryon Fieldbow. Sixty-four inches in length, weighing a total of twenty-five pounds... Perfect, isn't she?"

"You even have the quiver like bleedin' Robin Hood, in his later years, of course."

"I may be a man in my seventies, but I can hold me own."

"Are you sure about that? I saw you pull your back picking up a pen."

"Feck off, will ye? Ye want a go?" He pushes his glasses up on his sharp nose. I step closer to him, accepting the offer. He hands me the bow. I sometimes forget how big Jack is. Wide and heavy. A hulk of a man.

"How does this work?"

"First step, one foot on either side of the line I've drawn out. Here, take this arrow and place it on the rest and clip it to the string. Now pull it back and release."

I give it a go, aiming it at the target with the yellow dot in the middle. It's about twenty feet away. I release the bow and come up short. I give it another go and it ends up flying off the roof.

"Jaysus, I'm shite at this," I say.

"Let's hope nobody got hit down below."

"Why would you say that?"

"Here, I'll show you how the master does it." He grabs the bow out of my hand and before you know it he has three arrows shooting across the roof penetrating the yellow circle. All with ease and silkiness as if he's done this thousands of times. "Call yourself an assassin?"

"Yeah, with a gun or knife, not a feckin' bow and arrow."

"See, I'm a hunter at heart. I was born to kill," he says with his giant chest puffing out of his red polo shirt like a superhero.

"You work in a bike shop and sell guns on the side."

"What do you want?"

"What's wrong?" I say. "You're not still annoyed with me about the heist I did a few months back?"

"You lied to me. You said you were off to kill someone, not get yourself mixed up in a heist." He pushes me to the side.

"So it's okay to kill someone, but not rob some jewelry?"

"There's a difference between killing a rapist or child killer and going on a shambolic robbery where you could have got caught or, worse, killed."

"I needed to save Olivia, ye old fool."

"An old fool who could put an arrow in that mallet head of yours," he says slapping the tip of the arrow off my forehead. "Follow me, ye bleedin' eejit. I know you want something from me."

We climb down the ladder and go into the bike shop. Jack has a bit of a limp to his walk. The bike shop is more of a repair shop. Tools and bike parts are scattered here and there and there's a strong stench of oil and rubber.

"What are these?" I point at the boxes stacked high.

"Scooters… electric scooters. I bought a hundred of them from China."

"Those things are dangerous. I saw one of those delivery guys nearly get clipped by a bus."

"That's not my problem. I'll make a fortune from them. I might just stop selling weapons," he says with a tickled smile. He sits down in his swivel chair. He grabs his cane and holds it between his legs.

"I need something for the bike that can carry a large object."

"How large are we talking?"

"Something my size and weight."

"I only have that over there," he says, pointing with his cane. I take a few steps to the corner of the bike shop.

"Under here?"

"Yeah, pull it off." I yank up a blue tarp, and underneath it is a long trailer, red and bulky. "Five feet in length and can carry 160 pounds, enough to carry a body."

Let's hope this fella doesn't weigh much or I'm screwed. "It will have to do."

"I would help you, but I have a date this evening," he says.

"With who?"

"The nice lady who works at the florist down the road."

"Fair play."

"You could drag him around in a taxi," he says.

"So, you want me to drag a body around Dublin?"

"You could say he's drunk." We look at each other, knowing that plan won't work at all.

"I also need something for this," I say, pulling the dart from my pocket. He leans forward in his swivel chair, squinting his eyes. The chair makes a discomforting squeaking sound. He wipes his glasses with his thumb.

"What in God's name are you doing with a syringe dart?"

"I have to sedate the body that needs to go into that trailer," I say.

"These are rare. The only places you'll find them are veterinary clinics, farms, or zoos. I saw a video of a giraffe getting shot by a dart like this. Four thousand pounds in weight. Fell like a sack of potatoes."

"I need a gun of sorts. Do you have one?"

"For this, let me check in the back," he replies, struggling to get off the battered swivel chair. He puts all his weight on the cane and disappears in the shop.

"You should really get a new chair," I say. "The tape is peeling off."

"I can't find it," he shouts. "But I may have a contact for ye," he says to me with the phone nestled between his shoulder and head. "Let me make a quick call."

"I need water."

"Over there, in the corner." He nods to me. "Hello… I'm looking for someone by the name of… Dermot. It's urgent." He starts rooting through his desk drawer and removes a journal.

I give Jack a bemused stare as I lash back the plastic bottle of water, squeezing every last drop into my mouth. I once read the average human might consume forty-four pounds of microplastics in their lifetime from plastic bottles and seafood. If there's any truth to that statement, it's a frightening thought. "I need a Black Mamba," Jack says. "Very good." He hangs up the phone, tossing it on the desk.

"What was that all about?"

"My contact uses code words for different weapons. He'll meet you at the Hungry Tree in King's Inns Park in twenty minutes," he says.

"That was fast."

"This contact doesn't mess around. He'll be there bang on time."

"Did you order the right gun?" I ask.

"Haven't the slightest clue."

"But you ordered a Black Mamba," I say, perplexed.

"I'll have the trailer done in a couple hours. You can use that blue bike over there for the meantime."

"I better be off, then."

JACK MAGEE

CHAPTER TEN

It will take me twelve minutes to arrive at King's Inns Park. Using another bike doesn't feel right. I'm so used to my own, it almost feels like I'm cheating on it.

Sunday afternoon and the walking-tour groups are out and about. The double-decker tour buses are full and the hungover visitors wearing giant Guinness hats are spilling out of cafés and pubs after a late breakfast.

I even see a bunch of men wheeling suitcases and wearing checkered Scottish kilts of dark green, blue, and a hint of yellow. They have cans of Carlsberg in their hands and are singing songs. Not too far behind them is a group of women with pink bunny ears on their heads, coming out of a Mexican restaurant. Last night was rough for these lot and now it's time to go back home.

The puffy clouds above me are a perfect vanilla color, like scoops of ice cream, and I don't know if it's going to stay dry for the rest of the afternoon or snow. The battery on my phone is at 18 percent—I like to live life on the edge. I try texting Olivia to say I'm sorry I have to work. She hasn't read any of my text messages.

I roll down George's Street, barely pedaling, cutting through the rocky pavements of Eustace Street. Men and women with stretched earlobes, sleeve tattoos, and beanies on their heads stand outside a vintage clothing store smoking and vaping. I nearly hit a rail of used clothing with leather jackets.

Essex Quay. I cycle past the Viking longboat statue, which looks like the skeleton of a Viking ship buried halfway in the ground with three picnic tables in the middle. A flock of dirty pigeons nibble bread crumbs off them. One of them is fighting another with missing toes, absolute savages.

I take a right on Father Mathew Bridge, a three-span elliptical arch stone bridge with a rich history. I'm cycling north. My thighs are burning up and I might have to pull over to rest.

Church Street. I'm almost there. I can see the park in the distance. Then, out of the blue, a black Mercedes hearse pops out like a turtle's head poking out of its shell on Brunswick Street. Jesus Christ. A funeral on a Sunday, I've never seen such a thing.

There must have been fifty or so gloomy faces walking behind the car. It has a walnut coffin inside with the letters **MUM** in white flowers. It reminds me of my mother's funeral, but the difference is that nobody showed up at hers. Not even my dad showed his mug, the wanker. Yeah, I haven't seen him since he legged it on us when I was a young boy, but he could have paid his respects. I'm sure her name would have shown up in the obituaries or he would have heard from another family member of her passing.

Tears run down the faces of loved ones as they walk slowly, arms locked to one another, wearing black dresses and creased suits they've never worn before. There's always one bleedin' eejit who's not wearing all black, making him look out of place. A few of them are counting down the minutes to the after party to get their hands on the mini ham-and-cheese sandwiches and a pint.

I cycle behind the funeral until the crawling hearse makes its way to St. Michan's Church on Halston Street. I pedal hard up hill to the entrance of King's Inns Park. I cycle through the open black iron gates. There's a piece of paper that reads **WET PAINT** flapping in the wind against it.

The park is pleasing to the eyes and nostrils. The grass is cut with straight lines, creating dark and light shades of green. They look like swimming lanes that I want to dive right into.

At the very top of the park is the Registry of Deeds building. Each wing is flanked by caryatids made of Portland stone. I can see the entrance on the left wing. Cornucopia statues of bacchante with grapes and wine are on display. The greenish dome on top of the building is supported by tall columns.

I search the park hard for the Hungry Tree. I'm a fool. The thing is staring right at me to my left. The monstrous London plane tree is devouring an iron bench alive. My stomach growls. I leave my bike in the lush grass and stare at the tree. I massage my tight hamstring.

"Quite the spectacle," a man in his late fifties says, entering the gates. He walks closer to me. "That tree is around 80 to 120 years old." He's wearing chestnut shoes, tight black jeans, and a black zipper jacket.

"It's something else," I reply, half smiling.

"Poor bench didn't stand a chance," he says. He has a gray-and-white beard similar to mine. The dark hair on his head is tightly cut. He's a tall fella, handsome, and sounds like a man who comes from an educated background. He sits down on the bench that's being swallowed by the tree's trunk. "Lovely day, isn't it?"

"Sure is."

"So, you want a Black Mamba?" he asks, sitting up straight, hands on his knees.

"Yeah," I say.

"You must be a big Lakers fan," he says. I look down. I forgot I'm wearing the Lakers hoodie I bought yesterday.

"I watch them now and then. The time difference doesn't really help."

"I'm more of a Bulls fan myself, you know, when Jordan played," he says. "The good ol' days."

"I preferred Kobe."

"You know what?" he asks.

"What?" I respond, standing a couple of feet away from him.

"I never understood the death of Kobe Bryant."

"Why is that?"

"You're worth… what was it… a few hundred million dollars and he's taking a helicopter ride to his daughter's basketball game at his academy all the way out in some place called Thousand Oaks. Wouldn't it make sense to live closer to the academy and avoid jumping into a bloody helicopter? You got the money." He shakes his head. "Just buy a house down the road from the thing."

I really didn't want to get into a debate with this man on whether Kobe should have lived closer to his academy or not.

"I don't know. Maybe this is what the rich do… take helicopter rides like it's a taxi or a bus, and fellas like me and you will never understand," I sit down next to him. There isn't much room on the bench.

"But it's bloody common sense if you ask me." He unzips his jacket, reaches into the inside pocket, and removes a brown envelope, laying it down between us. He then stands up.

"It's very rare I get an order for the Black Mamba," he says, zipping his jacket back up.

"What about payment?"

"Tell Jack he owes me," he replies playfully, walking off with his hands in his pockets. I shove the envelope into my shorts pocket.

~~GUN~~

CHAPTER ELEVEN

After my visit to King's Inns Park, I head back to the bike shop. I walk in and find Jack lying on his back like a big ol' panda, tightening a bolt with a spanner. His hands are filthy and his gums are on full display as he twists the spanner.

"She's nearly done," he says, breathing heavily. His stomach goes up and down.

"You need a hand?"

"Lift me up." He reaches out his hand and I pull him off the floor. He's a heavy lump of a man. His T-shirt and shorts are grimy and his white beard is barbaric, as if he just came back from a village raid. I feel the blood rush to my face. Now I'm out of breath.

"The thing is huge, isn't it?"

"Let's hope that vintage bike of yours can hold it." The long trailer looks mad hooked to the back of my bike.

"Why don't you get your driver's license?" He grabs his wonky cane.

"I never really needed one for the city. And, besides, it's easier to escape a hit by bike."

"You're not wrong there. Remember that bloke you took out a few years back?"

"Which one?"

"The guy from the Liberties. He murdered his parents. It was a big deal at the time. He used a hand axe to kill them both. Feckin' lunatic. You said you took him out at his flat, but there was Garda in the area at the time."

"Oh yeah, I had two Garda cars hunting me down on Oliver Bond Street, but once I got to the quays, it was game over. They weren't catching me on those tight roads."

"I'm sure the traffic held them up good."

"Big-time. The funny thing was that the Garda pulled over a car later that day and found two hundred grand worth of drugs from the same apartment complex where I took out the axe man," I say.

"I was wondering why there was so many Garda chasing after ye."

"They were doing checkpoints in that area all day. They must have got a tip about a car filled to the rim with drugs."

"Imagine that. Being neighbors to a bloke who murdered two people with an axe," Jack says.

The bike shop door opens up. A couple in their mid-thirties comes breezing in. The both of them are clean and smell of rich perfume and cologne. The woman is wearing a green V-neck jumper, tight blue jeans, brown boots, and a long black military-style coat.

As for the partner, he's wearing toffee-colored corduroy trousers, shiny black shoes, and a dark gray coat buttoned all the way up. The handsome fella rolls in a bright-pink children's bike.

"How are ye?" the man asks. "We need someone to help us repair this bike."

"Our daughter's birthday is tomorrow and her bike arrived this morning broken," the woman says, sounding upset.

"How tragic," Jack says.

"The seat is loosened and the tire is flat," she says.

"I'm sure I can fix it," he says.

"Can it be done today? We really want to surprise her tomorrow morning."

"I close up soon," Jack responds, wiping his hand into a rag.

"We can pay you double." The man reaches into his pocket.

"That's not the problem," Jack says. "See, I have a hot date and I really want to go on—"

"Please, all the other bike repair shops are too busy. This is her big gift, she's been waiting months for it. All her friends will be there tomorrow. We even have a bouncy castle for the kids."

"Bad news, those things. Did ye not hear about the children in Australia who were swept away by a gust of wind inside a bouncy castle? Up they went, whirling in the air like they were a piece of litter, blowing down the road." He points his cane high above his head, hitting the light fixture.

The woman leans her neck forward like an ostrich. "What happened?"

Jack also leans in and whispers, "They all died, tragic. I'm sure I can fix this little thing." He takes the bike off the man's hands. "Look how dainty this is, Patrick. Come back in hour," he instructs the couple. They leave the bike shop confused.

"You're sick in the head," I say. "Why would ye say such a thing?"

"I'm just giving them a heads-up that accidents can happen."

I hop on my bike. The trailer weighs a ton. I won't be getting in any chases carrying this thing around the city.

"I'll have the trailer back to you tomorrow."

"Take your time and good luck with the hunt, and don't forget who taught you how to shoot," he says, holding the pink bike by the handlebar.

CHAPTER TWELVE

The distance between Camden Street and Airfield Estate is approximately seven kilometers, which is about a twenty-five-minute bike ride. With the massive trailer not fitting in the bike lane and taking up half the bloody road, it will be a miracle if I arrive at the Mansion House on time this evening.

I look at the time. It's four o'clock, and all I want to do is curl up beside Olivia and Simone, read my Carlo Goldoni play, and fall right asleep afterward. I'll need to make it up to Olivia later. I'm sure right now that she's throwing darts at a board with my ugly face on it.

A double-decker bus rudely overtakes me on Rathmines Road Lower.

"Bleedin' dope," the driver shouts out the window, his upper lip snarling in the side mirror. The roar of the engine is awful as the fumes spray out from the exhaust into my face. I cough into my elbow. The bike wobbles.

The road is bendy on Rathmines Road Upper and the traffic is horrendous. The trailer goes up on the curb, nearly hitting a fella carrying a sack of potatoes over his shoulder outside Tranquila Park.

I get few impatient fuckers beeping their horns from the vehicles behind me. I end up flying down a hill and taking a shortcut through Dartry Park.

The sun is shining exquisitely and for once the wind is calm and gentle on my body. On the paths I see a Yorkshire terrier with a black-and-tan coat running beside me with its tiny tongue sticking out. I hear the owner yell, "Princess, get back here!" The dog abruptly stops running. I look back and it gives me a stuttering bark, which I find adorable.

I cycle over a narrow bridge. The trailer scratches up against it. I really hope this thing doesn't snap on me and cause an accident. To my left is the Ely's Arch, built in the eighteenth century, similar to the India Gate in New Delhi or the Arc de Triomphe in Paris, but much smaller.

Braemor Road. I arrive at Churchtown Upper in one piece, without getting clipped or yelled at by any more drivers. I cycle past Dundrum shopping mall, which is utter mayhem and one big headache. The car park gives me anxiety.

Overend Avenue. I've reached my destination. Home to the Overend family since 1894, before it was handed over to the eccentric sisters Naomi and Letitia Overend. The estate is thirty-eight acres, with a farm, many gardens, a heritage experience, and a restaurant. The place is enormous. On my phone I download a map of Airfield Estate, which resembles a theme park.

I have a name, Ruby Collins, and a map. I don't know what he looks like and I don't have much time to find him to pierce his skin with a dart.

I cycle into the enchanting estate. To my left is the ticket box and to my right is the parking lot. I see families going to their cars. There's no security floating about, which is a good sign, but I'm sure there's enough staff members roaming the estate to catch me in the act.

To the far side of the parking lot is a gate surrounded by towering leafy trees. I head over and stop in front of the gate. I get off my bike. The gate is locked. I whip out my lockpick set and remove a tension wrench. I go to work on the lock and it opens without any problems.

I need to move quickly with the trailer before someone snitches on me. I throw my leg over the seat on the bike and cycle past a tiny pond. To my right are a bunch of fields with many sheep devouring the grass like vacuums.

I continue cycling straight and come to a large sign that reads **MILKING PARLOR**. I stop for a moment, feeling my shin splints acting up again. I hear a loud *moo* sound a couple of feet away from me. An immense brown cow stares at me with its penetrating black eyes and hairless wet nose. One of its ears wiggles.

I come across another sign: **JACOB SHEEP, OXFORD SANDY BLACK PIGS, SAANEN GOATS, RHODE ISLAND RED HENS, AND CHICKENS THIS WAY**. I leave the bike and trailer on the side of the path.

I walk over to an employee wearing a dark red T-shirt with the Airfield Estate logo. She's standing beyond the fence where chickens are getting chased by a gang of rowdy children.

"How are ye?" I ask the woman, who has a large forehead and sunglasses too small for her face. I lean forward. "I'm looking for a Ruby Collins…ye wouldn't happen to know where he's at?" I ask her in the most over-friendly way possible, with a fictitious smile that's straining my cheeks.

"Yes, I can help. He's located in the stables on the far side of the estate near the house," she replies, pointing, her fingernails coated in a vibrant blue polish.

"Thank you so much," I respond, bowing like an old Japanese man.

"No problems." The children form a circle around the woman, holding eggs in their little hands. I return to my bike, cycling over to the Airfield House. As I look around, I realize I should come here again with Olivia, if she ever forgives me.

The elaborate gardens ahead of me are truly magnificent. There's rows of elegant Malus "Evereste" trees and a pergola with roses and wisteria growing on it.

A subtle breeze comes blowing onto the crops in the organic food garden. To my far right is a sunken garden and the greenhouse garden. I cannot go farther with the trailer, so I leave it outside the front entrance of the Airfield House.

The two-story building is quaint, with a heavily castellated porch and a Gothic-style front door. I could easily see a wedding being held here. It's hard not to be distracted by this place. They even have vintage cars.

The Overend sisters have a garage with a 1927 Rolls-Royce and an Austin Tickford. The mother owned a Peugeot Quadrilette nicknamed the "The Flea."

So much history on such a pleasant day, but I must keep on track for this innocent man who will see the sharp end of a needle. I see an arrow directing me to the stables.

I look at the time: five o'clock. I walk toward the stables. I don't see anybody. No staff members on a smoke break or any blokes that look like a Ruby. With a name like that, he must be curious-looking. No average Joe goes by the name of Ruby, ridiculous.

I open the gate and close it behind me. I remove my leather gloves and make sure the dart gun is loaded with the tranquilizer. I stick the gun in my back pocket. The warm sun catches the side of my face.

Four horses are standing around eating hay. Then I see a majestic creature trotting out from the stables, a purebred Irish Connemara pony.

It's the exact likeness of the horse in the movie *Into the West*. Almost snow white with hints of gray to its coat. It has strong, muscular upper legs, defined cheekbones, and a mane that flows in midair as it hurries by me. I can't take my eyes off the horse.

I keep moving. I see the stables ahead and walk in. Of course, there's the sour smell of urine and the faint smell of manure, but that's expected. I'm getting a whiff of something burning. To my left and right are stalls, all filled with horses. I don't know the breeds of these ones. Two of them are a chestnut color, three of them black, and one that is buckskin with a white stripe down the middle of its face in the shape of a long spoon.

At the end of the stables is hay storage and across from it is a man sitting on a stool hammering a horseshoe on the hoof of a horse.

"Does it hurt him?" I ask, tiptoeing up behind the man. He removes the nails between his lips. The horse shakes its large head from side to side.

"Sorry?" he replies, blood rushing to his face as he turns to me. He's wearing a leather apron and has his shirtsleeves rolled up to his red elbows. He has a Jason Statham look to him. Short, bald, but stocky, with thick forearms.

"The horse, does he feel the nail going through his hoof?"

"He doesn't feel a thing," he says. "Once I give him a good trim, he's grand."

"I'm looking for someone."

"Who?" He stands, gripping the hammer in his hand.

"Ruby Collins."

"What do you want with him?"

"I need to see him," I say.

"I don't think you should be back here," he says.

"Why not?"

"Because you don't work here. Who are you exactly?"

"I just need to see Ruby Collins."

"You should leave." He shakes the hammer at me.

"Don't you point that thing at me."

"Get out now," he says, raising his voice. His bald head gets tense, veiny, and his face goes wrinkled as a fierce expression comes over him.

"Don't speak to me like that. I'm just looking for Ruby."

"What did I say? Get out!"

"No," I say. "Not until I see Ruby."

The stable falls silent except for the sound of a groaning horse behind me.

"Okay, you want to see him? I'll show ye. Follow me," he says, but I have a sneaky suspicion he's lying as he walks in front of me. Then he turns around, swinging the hammer my way. I fling my head back, falling backward as the hammer almost slices the tip of my nose off.

The bastard strikes again. I move to the side. Then a third time. This time I stop him by clutching his thick forearm before shouldering him hard in his eye socket. I shake the hammer out of his hand and kick it away from us. He touches his face. He's pissed now.

With his eyes turning oily black, he comes running toward me. My instincts take over and I hit him with a brutal flying knee to his head. I plummet backward, smashing my body against a stall. The man collapses to the ground next to me, as if I cast a frozen spell on him.

"Jesus Christ," I whisper to myself. I wonder if he's Ruby Collins. I root through his pockets. I remove a leather wallet from his side pocket. His driver's license reads *Eddie Bracken*. Slightly out of breath, I skim the stalls. There's a nail sticking out from the stall I fell into. I check the back of my hoodie. There's a hole in it, great.

I look around frantically. The clock is ticking. I notice each stall door has a name. **MOON STALLION, CURIOUS WINSTON, SHADOW GRACE**, and then I come to the name at the end: **RUBY COLLINS**. It can't be.

The stall seems vacant beyond the door. I poke my head over the stall and there's a gray miniature horse eating hay. Is this Ruby Collins? Does Nocturnal want me to tranquilize a miniature horse? It must be. I hear the Eddie fella on the ground, sprawled out and snoring.

I don't have much time. I remove the dart gun from my back pocket and aim it at Ruby Collins. I press the trigger and the dart shoots out, making a *pop* sound similar to a silencer, puncturing him in the backside. I throw the dart gun into a bin near me.

I wait a few minutes, watching Ruby eventually plummet to the ground. I hurry, wheeling the bike and trailer into the stables. I struggle to lift the miniature horse. He weighs a ton. His head is massive. It's not like picking up Simone. She's lean, half the size, and doesn't smell foul like Ruby.

The sky is getting dark and the air is much cooler. I look for a cover to hide the miniature horse. I find a thick blanket in the Moon Stallion stall. The only problem is the horse doesn't have kind eyes like the others. He's ready to kick my forehead.

I gently open the gate and go inside the stall. I pet him down. Then I make a move for the blanket. I pick it up, but the horse starts whinnying right in my ear. He kicks his back legs high up, smacking them viciously against the wall behind him. He puts a big dent in the stable. I leap over the gate, falling on my backside. I throw the blanket over Ruby, who's lying in the trailer. I get on my bike and start pedaling.

"He's stealing Ruby!" yells a woman in her late fifties at the entrance of the stable. I fly past her. Another one tries to block me at the exit. He shuffles from side to side like a defender playing basketball. I pedal fast toward him. His eyes light up. He dives to the ground. Dust shoots up in the air.

"Ye swine!" the woman shrieks, almost losing her voice.

~~RUBY COLLINS~~

CHAPTER THIRTEEN

I pedal my heart out, escaping Airfield Estate with just a scratch, which could have been a lot worse. I never thought I'd be defending myself from a farrier with a hammer, ready to take me out over a miniature horse.

Having said that, not so long ago I was attacked by a female dentist with a sharp dental tool. She struck me good in the shoulder and I still get the occasional shooting pain as a healthy reminder. I can't trust anyone.

I squint at the time on my phone. I have twenty-five minutes to get back into the city.

I'm pressing so hard on the pedals, it makes my quads hurt and forearms tense up. My hoodie is stuck to me. The miniature horse is heavy in the trailer. Let's hope kidnapping a miniature horse is what Nocturnal really fancied me doing all along.

As the night slithers in, so does the cold. It drops in temperature as I make my way on Goatstown Road in the narrow bike lane. I accidently clip a few plastic bollards. I look behind me. One of them is fully bent in half. Disaster.

I cycle onto the road. The strong streetlamps shine down on me and the miniature horse. With my arse off the seat, I use all the power in my forearms to grip the handlebars and weave the bike to overtake an orange 2003 Nissan Micra driving at a sloth's pace. I cycle past University College Dublin. Clonskeagh Hospital is to my left.

The bike journey takes me into Ranelagh, where there's heavy traffic. The pubs and restaurants are full.

My legs are tiring out now, but I have to keep pushing through the pain. My chest tightens as I make the turn on Harcourt Street. I'm almost there. I can see it from the corner of my eye. I hear the miniature horse squirming on the trailer like he's having a bad dream the way dogs do. Simone pops into my head. I miss her.

I think Ruby might wake up anytime now as I cycle over the tram tracks. The bike and trailer wobble. I arrive just on time. The Mansion House is located on Dawson Street. Built in 1710, it is the oldest freestanding house in Dublin. Queen Anne–style architecture, classical window frames, and at the main entrance a cast-iron canopy.

At the very top of the house is a central pediment with the city's coat of arms. It's of three watch towers—you'll spot it scattered throughout the city on litter bins and lampposts and in city hall.

Two minutes after six. I've made it. The round-faced security man built like a bull I saw earlier comes over to me as I pull up outside. I'm knackered.

"You're late," he says, nostrils broadening. I catch a whiff of his strong cologne, smelling like malt vinegar. He removes the blanket and leans down, picking the miniature horse up with ease like he's in a strongman competition. I lock the bike on a railing beside the building.

A flashy Bentley Continental GT V8, the color onyx black, pulls up on the cobbled forecourt outside the Mansion House. I recognize the model. I saw it last week advertised on a bus shelter.

A couple step out of the vehicle like they're walking onto a red carpet. The ol' fella is wearing a white tuxedo jacket and must be in his late sixties, and the woman looks to be in her early twenties. She's wearing a tight burgundy cocktail dress and black high heels. They enter through the blue door. I follow them.

When I walk into the entrance hall, a woman with a heart-shaped face, hair braided into a bun, greets me. "Champagne, sir?" she asks with a warm, endearing smile. She's wearing a three-piece black suit, white powder makeup, and red lipstick and holding a silver tray.

"Don't mind if I do." I take a sip of the bubbly. It has a hint of rosé to it. Very nice indeed. To my left is a marble chimneypiece. Above it hangs a painting of Daniel O'Connell, who was Lord Mayor of Dublin in 1841.

I move to the next room, the Lady Mayoress Parlor, also known as the Blue Room. I have the look of a small-time drug dealer, the way I'm dressed. I feel like I've been sent back in a time machine to the eighteenth century.

Everybody is dressed to impress in this room smelling of irritating perfumes and full of snobby faces. They all look like they have money to burn and are up to no good. It's all older men with younger women with luxurious jewelry that glimmers around their necks and dainty wrists.

I lash the rest of the champagne down my throat. It tickles. I'm not a huge fan of champagne, it gives me a very bad headache, but as an Irishman, it would be rude to refuse a free drink.

The Drawing Room is next. But, there's something different about this room. It has prints on these tall white walls like you see at an art exhibition. I take a closer look at the prints, placing my empty champagne glass on top of a piano.

The painting I observe is entitled *Le Cirque* by Georges Seurat and shows a female performer standing on a moving white horse. The horse is identical to the one I saw earlier at the stables. There's a creepy clown at the bottom of the painting who looks on in astonishment at the acrobats as they leap from the horse.

"What do ye think?" asks a voice behind me. I turn around, and standing straight as an arrow is Nocturnal. There's a woody odor to him. He's in a blue velvet suit with a white silk cravat tucked away in his shirt. The light fixture above our heads shines bright, bouncing off his perfectly round head.

"Is this an original?" I ask.

"You've quite the eye, Mr. Callen." Nocturnal takes a sip of his champagne. "A friend of mine has loaned it to me for the night." He stands closer to me.

"From the Musée d'Orsay?" I say. "This is worth a fortune."

"I hope you didn't run into any problems with Ruby Collins?"

"A stocky bald fella didn't seem too pleased."

"Ah, Mr. Bracken. He can be a handful. We had problems in the past with him. We stole another horse from him before."

"Why not buy one yourself?"

"Ruby Collins is a very famous miniature horse. He was in the circus for many years and he can do all sorts of tricks. My guests love him," he says with a sly smile. "Walk with me."

I stare at the other paintings in the room, passing *Acrobats at the Cirque Fernando* by Pierre-Auguste Renoir, *Miss La La at the Cirque Fernando* by Edgar Degas, and *At the Circus Fernando, the Rider* by Henri de Toulouse-Lautrec, but these are all prints, *Le Cirque* being the only original.

We end up in the Oak Room. It has Georgian-style crystal chandeliers produced by Waterford, rich plasterwork on the ceilings and the walls, and floors paneled with oak. The stuffy room is packed with people sitting down, staring at the stage, waiting. We stand in the back of the room as the lights dim.

"What's going on here?" I ask.

A strong light shines on the stage and a woman comes running out dressed as a ringmaster, with a top hat and everything, like it's *The Greatest Showman*. It's all too bizarre for my liking. I need to get home to Olivia—now.

"Jesus," I mumble under my breath. "I need to go."

"You're not going to stick around for the show?" He sounds disappointed.

"No, I'm good."

That's why I kidnapped a bloody miniature horse? Fuck me. This has to be one of the most outlandish jobs I've ever done, and I kill for a living. I make it out to the hallway feeling tired. I take a deep breath as I hear a round of applause from the Oak Room. Poor Ruby Collins.

At the main entrance, I see a fire alarm lever. And like a sly fox, I trot over and pull on it. The alarm goes off in the building and the sprinklers turn on above me. I pull my hoodie over my head. The water sprays on the walls, soaking the carpet, and drips down on the old paintings. I hear the howls of women. They come out in their glitzy dresses, tiptoeing, purses over their heads. I can feel the faintest of smiles form on my face.

~~THE MANSION HOUSE~~

CHAPTER FOURTEEN

I begin riding home on Dawson Street with the empty trailer still attached to the bike. The front wheel of my bike feels slightly deflated. The weight of the miniature horse probably didn't do it any good.

From the corner of my eye, I watch people go in and out of pubs and restaurants. Plans go out the window for some unlucky souls who say, *Let's go for a casual one or two pints, it's a Sunday, we have work tomorrow.* Then they find themselves five pints deep with two glasses of whiskey in their belly.

As I'm pedaling on Dawson Street, I feel the tires getting caught in the tracks. It's then I hear something loud, like the thunderous roar of an engine, like it's about to combust. I feel my whole body move with the bike as I'm struck from the back. I collide with two parked cars on the side of the road, slamming my body into them hard. Everything goes dark.

My eyelids struggle to open, as if they've been glued shut. Everything is blurry. I can't see shit. Everything is bright around me. I close my eyes tightly. I rub them, trying to get my bearings. My vison is coming back to me as I squint. I'm lying down on a hard bed feeling paralyzed.

"Where am I?" I mumble. I look down at my arm. There's an IV hooked up to me on the inside of my elbow. I pull the sheets down. I'm wearing a thin white gown. Where the fuck am I?

A pink curtain pulls sharply across in front of me. The hooks make a clinging sound. I get a fright. A towering woman in her forties appears with a clipboard in her hand. Her shoulders are wide and round beneath her blue scrubs. "Where am I?" I ask again, feeling anxiety come over me like I've woken up from a bad nightmare.

"You're at the hospital, of course," the woman replies, checking on the IV system. Her dark hair is in a milkmaid braid and she has long scratch markings on her neck as if she has been clawed by her cat recently.

"Which one?" My mouth feels dry and disgusting.

"St. Vincent's."

"How did I end up here?" I rub my forehead in a circular motion and feel the swelling of a tiny bump protruding from my skin.

"You were in a bike accident, Patrick." She writes down something on the clipboard. "Apparently, a vehicle hit the trailer attached to your bike, flinging you right off. It was quite the scene. Luckily, a couple walking by called an ambulance." I try to lift myself up, but my body is so tender and fragile. "Easy now, Patrick. You suffered a concussion and bruised up your hip pretty badly," she says. I get the whiff of Chanel perfume as she leans over me, adjusting my pillow. I recognize the scent. It's the same one Olivia uses. "You're lucky you didn't get killed, the driver that hit you took off into the night."

"What's in the IV?"

"We have you on a low dosage of morphine for your hip pain. There doesn't seem to be any other injuries except for the bump on your head. Stop worrying, Patrick. You just need some rest, and keep hydrated, okay?"

"Where's my phone and wallet?"

She responds by pointing with her pen at the bedside table.

"There will be food coming around shortly. I'll be back in an hour to check on you." She pulls the curtain across. I can see her white New Balance trainers under the curtain as she leaves. I grab my phone from the bedside table. The battery is dead and the screen has a crack in the corner.

I pull the bedsheet to the side. The pain in my left hip is excruciating. I lift my gown up carefully, and there it is, a massive bruise the size of a flat crepe and the color of crushed blueberries smeared across my hip bone, thigh, and buttocks.

My body feels like it's been flung up in the air and run over by a bull, like those eejits do in Spain every year. Running of the Bulls, I think it's called.

I need to call Olivia immediately. She needs to know where I am and that I'm safe.

My clothing is neatly folded on a chair to my right. I see no windows. I shift my body out of the bed, yanking the IV out of my arm. It stings as if I've ripped off a viper. I stand up, barefoot. but have to sit back down. My legs are jelly.

The IV machine is having a meltdown beside me. I need to move fast. I put my clothes on, grab my wallet, phone, and keys. I slip into my slippers and gently pull the curtain across, looking around the warm, stuffy room, which houses two other beds.

The Seiko clock on the wall near the entrance reads a little after eleven. Olivia is going to kill me. I look to my left, and my bike is leaning up against an old radiator. It's still in one piece, having survived the crash. I start wheeling it out of the room.

I hear something close to me. I turn my head, peeking through the curtains. I hear a husky voice: "I wouldn't leave if I were you." An old man, thin and decrepit in a wrinkled gown, is standing in the dark with the whites of his eyes on show. I can see half his face. I don't respond to him.

I glance left and right out in the hallway like I'm crossing a busy main road. I make a left, moving with speed and determination, hoping nobody spots me fleeing like a fugitive. I get into an elevator, pressing the ground-floor button.

The pain punches me in the hip as I throw my leg over the bike and start pedaling on Merrion Road, which will take me all the way into the city. The sky is black, cold, starless. I feel alone as I slowly pedal in agony. I need to get home to Olivia. I know she's going to be mad, but I need to fix it.

The mirror attached to the handlebar is smashed, not helping matters. I'll need to visit Jack. As for the trailer, who knows where that is. I eventually arrive in the city. The streets are awfully quiet. I can hear myself breathing heavily as the wheels rotate.

I arrive in Smithfield Square, which is lifeless, with end-of-the-world vibes. I enter my building and gaze at the older lady sitting at the front desk and eyeing me up and down with her hands clenched in a raised position near her face. I step into the elevator, reach my floor, and limp to the loft. When I enter, the lights are off.

Simone is on the couch resting. It's late. Her energy levels are low. I leave my bike against the wall. The dog's tail swipes left and right as I come closer to her, petting her head.

"Where's Olivia?" I ask her, like she's going to respond. "Olivia," I shout out as I walk up the stairs gripping the handrail.

She's not in the bed or in the bathroom. Where the devil is she? I go back down the stairs, panicking. Simone is slurping on her bowl of water. I remove my phone from my pocket, connecting it to the charger. My eyes dart around the room without blinking. I turn the lights on. Then I see it, a piece of paper on the kitchen countertop.

I pick it up and begin reading. *"Patrick, I can't do this anymore. I can't take the lies."* My heart sinks as I collapse to the floor. I lean back against the kitchen cabinet and thump my fist on the floor. I feel a stabbing pain in my hip, now coming in waves. I reach for the freezer and remove a bag of frozen baby carrots, placing it on my bruised hip. I read the note again, taking in deep breaths.

Olivia is gone. She's left me.

CHAPTER FIFTEEN

I wake up in the pitch darkness of the loft, hoping Olivia's warm body is going to be lying next to me in the bed. Stretching out my arm, I feel nothing but cold bedsheets. I hear Simone jump off the end of the bed, her sharp nails scraping the floor as she begins limping downstairs. Even the dog wants nothing to do with me.

I check my phone. Three in the morning. The brightness on my phone stings my eyes. I'm exhausted. The temptation to text Olivia is killing me. All I want to do is apologize and tell her she means everything to me and that she's the most important person in my life. I call her number but it goes straight to voicemail.

The pain in my hip is worsening. The melting bag of baby carrots hasn't done much but made the bedsheets damp, like I've just wet the bed. I need something strong to relieve the pain. It's impossible to get any sleep. Even when I try to lay my body on one side, the other side gets numb and stiff.

I scroll through my contacts to the letter C. I press on the name Clodagh. The phone rings out. Come on, you, I know you're awake.

"Hello," the woman shouts in a thick cockney accent. I can hear loud rock music blasting away in the background.

"It's Patrick," I say, almost yelling in pain as I lift myself off the bed.

"I know that, sure didn't your name pop up on me screen, you twat," she says, sounding her usual cheeky self. "What do ye want?"

"I need drugs. Something strong."

"Weren't you a drug addict?"

"Yes, but I got in a bike accident recently and my hip is bruised up badly."

"Not my problem. Go to a doctor."

"You are a doctor."

"I used to be a doctor, get it right."

"Come on, don't be like this. I'll give you some money," I say. There's silence on the phone. I've got her attention.

"Two hundred euros," she says.

"One hundred."

"I'm going to hang up."

"Okay, okay, relax that big head of yours. I'll be over now, give me fifteen minutes."

"Now?" she says. I hang up the phone.

I have a warm shower and get dressed in fresh clothing, navy-blue shorts and a plain white T-shirt. My body is aching in pain as I put my arm through the sleeve of my dark-red hoodie. The bruise on the inside of my elbow is green and pale yellow. I've always bruised easily, even as a young fella, but as you get older the skin gets thinner, more fragile.

I throw all my dirty clothing in the washing machine, adding Lenor liquid detergent to it, and press the quick-wash button. The back of my neck is soaking wet from my long hair dripping down. I rub Simone's big floppy ears as she lies on the couch with sadness in her eyes.

I put my slippers on and push my bike out of the loft and start pedaling slowly, in pain, on the quays. It feels strange cycling at this time of night. The streets are deserted and the city feels like it's in a coma.

I swing a right over O'Connell Bridge, built between the years 1791 and 1794. The bridge is wide to help with traffic congestion and has great views of the river Liffey. It's only recently I've noticed the decorative three-armed five-lantern lamps, which resemble something on the streets of Paris.

I make a wincing right on Lombard Street, pressing on my hip as I pass the Windjammer pub. I've finally made it to Boyne Street. I lock me bike across the road next to a dead pigeon and walk over to what looks like a row of abandoned garages, with green foliage and vines growing on the roof and rusty barbed wire. The caged windows are like something you see on a prison.

I give the metal door a good walloping, scoping the area around me, making sure some chancer doesn't have any ideas about stabbing and mugging me, because that's how the street feels right now. Or maybe that's just my paranoia kicking in.

I see a shadowy figure approaching at the bottom of the door. The light flickers as if the bulb is loose.

"Clodagh!" I yell out. The door opens. Standing in front of me at five foot nothing is disgraced doctor Clodagh Watson. Known for working with gangsters in Ireland years ago. She stares up at me, not saying a word, just disgusted to see my face show up at her so-called doorstep.

She's wearing a fitted white vest and baggy jeans with holes in them and has a menacing pixie haircut. Though she has massive leather boots on, she still short as shit, but I'm sure she could put up a fight against the best of them.

"You really know how to put me in a mood, don't ye?" she says. I push my way inside, not wasting any time.

"I need a painkiller, I'm a wounded beast." I'm holding my hip like an old lady who slipped and fell on some black ice.

"Lie down. Let me see what I have for ye in the kitchen."

"It smells like shite in here." There's a mural of Jimi Hendrix on the brick wall to the far right of the garage. I plop myself down on a weathered green couch, which I'm pretty sure she sleeps on.

"Here, drink this." She hands me a shot of bourbon. I swallow it back as she places pillows under my feet. "I'll get you an ice pack for the hip." Clodagh heads back to the kitchen area. I take a look around and see empty bottles of vodka and whiskey on the coffee table in front of me. The floor is concrete and cold and has greasy footprints.

"It's freezing in here," I say to her.

She throws an ice pack at me. "Put it on your hip for twenty minutes, then take it off for twenty minutes and then back on again, understand, dummy?" She's now on her knees beside me. "I have ten pills of tramadol, it's the only thing I could find in my cabinet. You take one every four to six hours." She's holding a pill bottle between her thumb and index finger. She starts shaking the container at me. The pills rattle inside. I reach out but she pulls away. "Payment first."

I reach into my pocket and hand her two hundred euro cash. I swallow back one pill. I haven't had this sensation in over ten years. There was a time I was addicted to these little things.

I used to live on the Northside of Dublin in my twenties, cleaning the floors in a filthy chipper. I would rush home, swallow some pills, and fall asleep to the Beatles, which my roommate played all day and night as I lay in bed strung out on pills.

"Pinball Wizard" by the Who is playing on a low volume as I rest my eyes on the couch.

"Knock off that lamp," I say.

"You're not staying here tonight," she replies. Those are the last words I hear as my body shuts down.

CHAPTER SIXTEEN

Monday. My eyes start opening up. They feel dry and crusty on the corners. I give them a rub, slowly sitting up on the green couch, which is soaking wet with the ice pack. I look at the time on my phone. A little after twelve.

The metal door swings open to my left, and Clodagh struts in with a vape pen dangling for dear life between her lips. She's holding three heavy plastic bags. I can see the muscles tense up in her thin forearms. She dumps the bags on the floor, removes something under her armpit, and throws it at me.

"Eat up," she says, blowing out vape smoke that smells of fruit punch.

"What is it?"

"Breakfast roll," she replies. She picks the bags up from the floor and heads out to the back where the wheelie bins are. I unwrap the paper and dig into my roll, which has two bacon rashers, two sausages, an egg, and two white puddings. I remove the puddings, wishing Simone was beside me to gobble them up.

I'm starving. It's not too long before the breakfast roll is consumed and my belly is full. My hands are greasy as I lash back a glass of water along with my pill.

The good news is my hip is slowly healing. Clodagh yells out to me, "Come over here." I drag myself off the couch and go to the back of the garage. A chilly breeze sucker punches me in the face as I rub my arms, shivering.

"What's going on here?" I ask her as she fills a Teeling whiskey barrel with water from a leaky green hose.

"Pass me a bag of ice," she says. I give it to her.

She turns off the hose, cuts the bag open with her keys, and starts dumping the ice into the barrel. I keep passing her the bags until they're gone.

"Strip down," she says.

"What do you mean *strip down*?"

"You need to jump in the barrel." Clodagh gives me more of an order than a suggestion. "Don't you want to heal fast?"

"Yes, but that looks fuckin' cold." The thick ice cubes are floating miserably on the top of the water like crystals. I can hear some cracking.

"That's the point. Come on, now, clothes off."

I strip down to my undies. I step on a milk crate, dipping my toes into the barrel. I instantly get a shock through my body like I've been electrocuted. "It's bleedin' freezing." I take in deep breaths, throwing my legs in and pushing my body down deeper into the barrel. The water spills over as I dunk my shoulders lower in the water. I'm trembling as the ice cubes fall on the ground beside Clodagh's feet.

"Three minutes," Clodagh holds her watch close to her face, checking the time. "This will help with your bruising and any muscle pain you have." I try closing my eyes and taking in deep breaths.

Olivia drifts into my head. I see her on the balcony back at the loft, smoking, staring out at Smithfield Square. I see tears rolling down her soft cheek. I call out her name but there's no response.

Then my eyes open up.

"How many minutes are left?" My teeth are rattling.

"One more." My body is going numb. I need to get out. "All done." I launch my body up like a blue marlin. My private parts have shriveled up and disappeared back into my body.

Clodagh hands me a towel as I step out of the barrel, juddering and dripping everywhere. "You'll be running around before you know it." She slaps me hard on the back, looks down at her wet palm, and wipes it on her vest.

Who would have thought this one was a doctor at one point?

I quickly dry myself and get back into my clothing. I grab my phone and give Olivia a quick text: *Hi, when can we meet up and talk?* The message is delivered but she hasn't seen it yet. Fingers crossed she gets back to me soon. I already miss the woman.

"Thanks for the help." I put on my slippers, getting ready to leave. "I'll see you around."

"Hopefully not." The tiniest of smiles appears on her face.

I get on my bike with great difficulty. The bike needs some repairing. The mirror on the handlebar is cracked, the black paint on the frame is peeling off, and there's a tear on the brown leather seat. The bike and I are both banged up.

I start cycling on Kildare Street, passing the National Library of Ireland, pushing through the pain in my hip. A large banner of Ireland's most famous poet, William Butler Yeats, is tied to the railings. Just like James Joyce, he too is giving me daggers through his fancy spectacles. The streets are packed with government buildings as I make my way swiftly on Earlsfort Terrace.

I cut through the car park of the National Concert Hall with ease, squeezing my bike into the back entrance of Iveagh Gardens. I love this delicate little park with its angel fountains, greenery, tall trees, and impressive waterfall.

I reach the other side of the park. The traffic is dreadful on Camden Street as I pass Devitt's pub on the corner. The Victorian building, established in 1871, is in a prime location. The top half of the building is redbrick and the bottom half is painted navy blue.

They even have an old Guinness advertisement on the side of the building of a workman in denim overalls standing on the nose of a seal, clutching a large clock. Is he fixing the thing or stealing it? A toucan is perched on top of the clock, chilling with a Guinness placed on its beak.

I approach the bike shop, swinging my leg over the seat, gently getting off. I lock it outside around a lamppost. As I get closer to the bike shop I notice the main entrance door is half-open.

"Jack," I shout out, but there's no response. The door makes that horrible creaking sound as I poke my head into the bike shop. When I enter I see Jack's cherrywood walking stick lying on the floor next to his desk, which I find rather unusual. He must be on the roof practicing his stupid archery again.

He's really asking for trouble shooting arrows off the bloody roof. He could kill someone or fall off it. I'm getting riled up.

I go back outside and climb the ladder on the side of the building. I reach the top and there's no sign of Jack. I try calling him on my phone. Nothing. I see a seagull squealing on top of a chimney.

I go back into the bike shop. I'm puzzled. Where the feck is he? He wouldn't leave the bike shop door open like this in the middle of the day. Something feels off.

My phone vibrates in my pocket. Jack's name shows up on the screen. Finally. I answer.

"Jack, where the feck are ye?" I ask him. "I need me bike fixed today."

"That's such a shame, because this isn't Jack," replies a man on the other end. His voice sounds malevolent.

"Then who is this?"

"You can call me the Bison," he says.

"Why do you have Jack's phone?"

"Let's just say I'm borrowing Jack for a bit."

"Who the fuck is this and what have you done with Jack?"

"Ah, relax, Patrick, he's doing grand... for now. Like I said, I've borrowed Jack until you complete a job for me."

"Why?"

"Because if you don't, I'm going to torture your close friend until he bleeds out." My mouth goes dry and I feel light-headed.

"What do you want me to do?"

"Just make sure your phone is fully charged today because I'll be sending you a name and location very soon."

"And what am I supposed to do with this name?"

"I want this person dead. That's enough for now. Talk soon, Patrick." The phone hangs up. I'm stunned as I fall back into Jack's banged-up swivel chair wrapped in silver duct tape. I feel as though I've been tased in the chest.

I squeeze my forehead, pushing my thumb in deep, feeling the shape of my skull. I stand up and look around the shop to see if there are any clues left behind. I take a gander in the back room, but there's nothing to see.

I search through the drawers, which are filled with bolts and screws. I pull on the last drawer. Inside is a wooden box with gold locks you would see on a vintage briefcase. I place the box on my lap, flicking the locks. I open it and inside is a .44 Magnum revolver. The words *Smith & Wesson* are engraved on the long barrel, resembling every bit of Dirty Harry's gun. Black in color with a wood grip. The weight feels foreign in my hands, heavy, like I'm holding a brick.

I shove the box with the gun inside a plastic bag lying on the floor. There's ammo in the drawer too, which I add to the bag. I look around the bike shop one last time, flipping over parts and making a bigger mess. Gazing up at the ceiling, I see something in the corner. I pull the swivel chair over and stand on it, which is probably a stupid move. It wobbles. I really hope I don't fall off and break my neck.

I stretch out my two arms like I'm about to change a light bulb and snatch the object off the tiny shelf. It's a security camera, a cheap one you can buy online for under fifty euro. I flip it over and remove the SD card from it and leave the bike shop, grabbing the plastic bag with the gun and ammo. I pick up Jack's walking stick and lean it against the desk.

My head is scrambling. I look at my phone. Still nothing from Olivia or this Bison fella. I turn the sign over on the door to **SORRY, WE'RE CLOSED, BE BACK SOON!**

Fuckin' Mondays.

CHAPTER SEVENTEEN

As I'm about to cycle, my phone starts vibrating in my pocket. I get a little nervous and queasy. I stare at the screen. Caitríona. What does she want?

"Hello," I yell over the engine noise coming out of a 1990 Yugo 55.

"Where ye at?" Caitríona asks.

"What happened to saying hello, how are things? You know, like normal people do."

"I don't have the time of day for small talk over the phone. Meet me at Dartmouth Square in one hour," she says.

"Jesus, okay. I'll be there—" Caitríona hangs up the phone before I can say my last word. Ruthless that one.

The agonizing pain continues in my hip as I start cycling on the canal, heading toward the Ballsbridge area. I glance at the bizarre United States embassy, which looks massively out of place, resembling something you would find in a Salvador Dalí painting.

Anglesea Road. I lock my bike outside Pembroke Library, built in 1927. It's a small library with a pediment bay that has an inset arch and round window similar in appearance to a dart board. Three rounded windows are on both sides of the building's main entrance and the roof has a small but impressive copper cupola.

I walk in, greeted by a man who is the spitting image of Stephen King. Arching over the front desk like a cat, he's wearing a loose-fitting red shirt and reading *Animal Farm* by George Orwell.

"Afternoon," he says to me, using a receipt as a bookmark.

"How are ye?"

"Grand, yourself? Looks like it's going to rain out there. It's been itching to all afternoon," he says.

"I wouldn't be surprised. I just want to use one of your computers, if that's okay with ye?"

"That's no problem," he says. "It's been very quiet. Pick any of them, the floor is yours." The man has a big smile on his face.

"Thanks."

The computers are next to the History section of the library. I've never seen so many spines with the name Hitler on them. I sit down, placing the plastic bag on the floor with the revolver inside. I remove the SD card from my pocket and stick it in the slot of the computer.

The SD card has thirty days' worth of recordings. I only saw Jack Sunday afternoon to get the trailer attached to my bike, so he must have been taken not too long after that. I click on yesterday's recording, fast-forwarding the footage. Jack repairs two bikes, which takes him a couple of hours, then eats Chinese food. I recognize the restaurant on the takeaway bag.

Then I slow it down to half five in the evening. Jack is putting on a fresh shirt and a pair of jeans. He must be getting ready for his date with the lady who works at the florist down the road.

It's around this time I would have been delivering a feckin' miniature horse to the Mansion House. Then it happens. Two fellas wearing balaclavas come rushing in, pulling Jack off his swivel chair. Jack tries to put up a fight, but they manage to drag him out of the bike shop. The bike shop falls silent. And what's left behind is his cane.

The video footage is harrowing. It's not pleasant viewing to see your best friend dragged away. God only knows what condition he is in. I rewind the footage multiple times to see if I can catch anything I've missed. It happens all too quickly and I can't get my head around the whole situation.

Who would do such a thing? Yes, I've murdered scumbags in my years as a hit man and threatened a long list of toerags, which they all deserved, but to do this? Now they want me to kill for them.

I remove the SD card and pick the plastic bag up from the floor with the gun inside. The bloke who is sitting at the front desk has his eyes closed and mouth wide open. There are a few cobwebs hanging around the library, and it would be no surprise if a spider ended up crawling in his mouth.

I stop at the drinking fountain at the entrance and remove the pill bottle from my pocket. I swallow back one pill and drink from the fountain. My hip stings as I bend forward. The old man lets out a robust snore.

Dartmouth Square by bicycle is only eleven minutes away. The weather is holding up, just about. I take my time. The flashing images of Jack getting hauled out by those two hoodlums make my stomach squirm. My mouth feels vile from the breakfast roll I ate earlier. The aftertaste of egg yolk lingers in the back of my throat.

On the way, I cycle past two junkies screaming at one another on the road. I nearly run over the chap, who looks like a scarecrow strung out on drugs. He keeps yelling, "Debbie! Debbie!" The woman has her tummy exposed as she swings her bruised arms about. She yells back, "Shut up, will ye!"

The houses surrounding Dartmouth Square are impressive and probably hover around the two-million-euro price tag. The Victorian garden square is charming, with mature trees and original wrought-iron railings and gates, which have been recently coated with fresh paint.

I cycle in, now feeling the heat. The hoodie is stuck to me skin. The air is humid and I wouldn't be surprised at all if the rain comes pouring down in the next hour. I do a lap inside the square on the stony walkway with the plastic bag hanging from the handlebar.

Slowly I pedal my bike. To my left I see a mixed bunch of characters doing yoga on the grass. Their bodies stretching, bending, in tight clothing. I try to remember the last time I could touch my toes. The hip injury is torture, so I get off my bike and start walking with it, breathing in the warm air, which makes me want to cough.

"Patrick." I hear someone speak under the pergola centered in the square. Caitríona is leaning against a pillar holding a leash. Attached is a French bulldog, gray with big bat-like ears and a wrinkled face. There's a plastic cone around its neck resembling a white buttercup.

"What happened to your dog?" I ask her.

"He got his balls removed." She emerges from the shadows wearing a black waistcoat with white stripes.

"Why?"

"He had a tumor, poor thing."

"I have a dog meself, great companions. They really do put a smile on your face."

"Are you all right in the head?" She wasn't lying about the small talk. "I have a job for you." I clear my throat, wiping my clammy hands on my shorts, and lean the bike against the pillar. She hands me a folded piece of paper.

"Who is this?" I open it up. The dog is sniffing my slippers.

"Sammy 'The Sleeper' Jenkins," she says. "Up-and-coming mixed martial artist from Inchicore. The address of where he trains is below the picture."

"What's his deal?"

"I know the Ukraine war has been stealing the headlines recently, but if ye turn a few pages over in the papers, there's a piece on this runt causing trouble in town."

"What's he been doing?"

"Last month he drop-kicked some young fella for bumping into him at a nightclub. Then he clipped someone with his sports car at a car park outside Tesco. He ended up paying them off, but that's not the worst of it, he choked out a sixty-year-old man at a pub."

"Running amuck by the sounds of things."

"You could say that. He's made a bit money and now he thinks he can do whatever the fuck he wants. The wife of the man who got choked out came to me the other day. She said her husband spent the night in the hospital." Caitríona shows me a photo of the man's neck on her phone.

"That's a nasty bruise," I say.

"She was livid and wants the young fella to pay for what he's done."

"How much she offering?"

"Three grand to give the boy a few digs and a warning. I'll give ye five hundred for this job," she says.

"Make it a grand," I say, my body feeling sticky and uncomfortable.

She waits a few seconds to reply.

"Seven hundred," she says. I nod in agreement. "The woman is a nervous wreck, so the sooner you sort this out the better."

"I might see this Sammy fella today," I say. "How did opening night go at the Crazy Owl?"

"It actually went well, a full house. It'll make way more money than that dump she was running before."

"She loved that dump," I say.

"It's a shame you didn't pay a visit," she says. "Heard you have a girlfriend." I nod. "I'm meeting a lovely woman meself," she says, reading her watch, "in about ten minutes."

"You better get going."

"She's meeting me here in this square."

"I was wondering why you wanted to meet me here."

"I might as well get two tasks done in one shot. Collecting the dog from the vet and meeting this young one. In all honesty, I could've just texted you over the details," she says. I shake my head. "What do ye think?" She shows me a picture of the woman she's about to meet up with.

Down at my feet, the bulldog looks strung-out on drugs like those junkies I saw earlier on the road.

"Attractive," I say, keeping my eye on the dog.

"Let's hope she's better-lookin' in person. Ye can't trust nobody these days. Not with all this catfishing that goes on."

"Is he all right?"

"He's just tired from the surgery. The anesthesia is wearing off him. He'll be brand-new by tomorrow," she says. The dog's eyelids are nearly shut. He doesn't look in good shape. A few seconds go by and he vomits beside my foot, almost getting my new slippers.

"Jaysus," I say. Caitríona removes something from her waistcoat pocket and begins spraying it into her mouth. It smells minty.

"Ah, here she is now, I better be off. I'll see you at the criminal courts tomorrow for payment." She pulls the leash hard. My phone vibrates in my pocket. Olivia's name pops up on my screen. I inhale and exhale out my mouth.

"Hello," I say gently, calmly, hoping she is the same.

"Patrick... how are you?"

"I was going to ask you the same thing."

"We need to talk. Meet me at four tomorrow in Merrion Square. Don't be late."

"Okay... sounds good. See you then."

She doesn't respond and hangs up. The phone call felt bitter, like a shot of apple cider vinegar.

"Come on, Bowie," Caitríona says to the dog.

When I take a closer look at my phone, I see a text message has been delivered. I click into it. It's from Jack's phone. The message reads: *Lorcan Doyle. Hint: Milltown Golf Club. Dump his body on the Dodder. You have until midnight or Jack dies.*

My chest tightens again and I grab a handful of my beard. I lean against the pillar in the shade, removing my notebook from my pocket. I begin writing a to-do list. My brain is fried.

TO-DO LIST

KILL LORCAN DOYLE

SAMMY "THE SLEEPER" JENKINS

MERRION SQUARE PARK

THE CRIMINAL COURTS OF JUSTICE

CHAPTER EIGHTEEN

I set a countdown on my phone for nine hours like it's a bomb about to fuckin' detonate. I don't have much time to being pondering about with my head up my arse. First things first, we have a name and a location, which is better than nothing.

Something feels so wrong about carrying a gun around in a plastic bag, like I just bought fresh milk and a loaf of bread. I hop on my bike, avoiding the puddle of vomit the dog left behind, and start traveling back toward Grantham Street.

I arrive at the location, which is only down the road from Dartmouth Square. I lock my bike outside a busy pasta bar. Next door is a large mural spray-painted with the words **U ARE ALIVE**. I pop into the pineapple-yellow charity store on the corner.

An African bloke struggles to lift a wide dresser out the front door. He reverses like a delivery truck with his ass crack exposed from his joggers for the world to see. Droplets of sweat roll down the side of his face and the back of his bright orange Ivory Coast football jersey has damp patches.

"Rock the Boat" by the Hues Corporation is playing as I walk into the stuffy store. It sells everything. To my right is an old-fashioned red and mustard-yellow couch with white tassels at the bottom. Beside the couch is a 1930s Singer sewing machine in great condition.

There're rails of old clothing that show wear and tear. Most likely someone died in them. With the cost of living rising there's no surprise the charity store is filled with lively, musky people on the hunt for a bargain.

There're broken lamps, old picture frames, chipped chairs, and a big TV that is about twenty years old. At the back of the shop they have scratched CDs, model trains, antique spoon and fork sets, cheap jewelry, board games probably missing pieces, and boxes of vinyl from the sixties. All of them one-hit wonders. The only good thing in the shop is the secondhand books.

There's a whole shelf with James Patterson novels. Below that are the usual suspects: John Grisham, Michael Connelly, Patricia Cornwell, Lee Child, Karin Slaughter, and Harlan Coben. I do a lap around the store and come across a basket filled with weathered handbags. I rummage through the pile. I pick up something from the bottom. In my hand is a fanny pack with a main-pocket zipper and a front zip pocket, still intact.

I once strangled a young woman to death with a fanny pack. She killed her mother by putting poison in her soup. She spent six years in prison, and when she got out, her brother wanted her dead.

I occasionally get flashbacks of her sneaking up behind me in her kitchen, trying to chop me in half with a cleaver. The sharp blade nine inches long, shining, with the woman's eye peeking through the little hole near the corner. She was the size of an elephant seal. Her arms jiggled with each strike. I couldn't get me gun out fast enough.

She came close enough to slicing the tip of my nose off. She struck again, almost carving my stomach out and leaving my entrails on the black-and-white tiles.

I let her use up all her energy before I finally made my move. I clutched her wrist, pulled her toward the floor, and shook the cleaver out of her hand. She was breathing profusely, as if she was going to pass out. I threw her on the floor, her face planted onto the tiles. I snatched the fanny pack off the kitchen countertop and wrapped it around her neck like I was roping a calf. My knee dug into her back and I squeezed so tight that my whole body tensed up. She let out a trumpet sound. I'd never heard that before when choking out someone.

Then there was silence. She was dead on the floor. I stood up in the hideous kitchen. The cabinets were all coated Barbie pink and the ceiling was covered in brown water stains.

I was curious about why she had a fanny pack on her. So I opened it up and found dozens of pills. I was only a year off pills at the time. The temptation to lash back five of them was unreal.

Now, inside a charity shop that has the lingering, suffocating odor of varnish and floral perfumes, I hold the fanny pack in my hand. I pay five euro to the old lady behind the counter for the thing. I wrap it around my waist, which feels much better.

There's an alleyway around the corner from the store. I remove the coffin-like box from the plastic bag, open it up, and take out the gun. I put it in the fanny pack along with the bullets, my keys, phone, leather gloves, and bottle of pills.

I hike back on my bike with my fanny pack around my waist. I feel a tad light-headed. The pills are kicking in, and the fasting is catching up to me. I really don't know how I'm going to have the energy to pull off this hit.

I type the words *Milltown Golf Club* into the map app on my phone. It's a fifteen-minute cycle. I begin my journey on Ranelagh Road. The sky is getting dark in the distance and it continues to be humid. Ranelagh village is lovely and tidy. There's trendy restaurants and pubs to have your pick from.

I find myself tensing up every time I think of the bastards who took Jack. I need to focus on the goal at hand. I pedal the bike over Classon's Bridge on Churchtown Road Lower, passing the Dropping Well pub. The river Dodder flows under me. It has a coldness to it that gives me the shivers. I have to do a double take when I see a bronze sculpture of a bleedin' African rhino in the river.

Churchtown Road Lower and I'm getting closer to the golf course. I see the car park up ahead. I get off my bike and lock it around a ramp sign. The clubhouse is a big building and looks more like a secondary school than a clubhouse. Above the main entrance it has a crest of a lion holding a sun, similar to the one on the Argentinean flag, with the year 1907 underneath it.

I walk in, and to my left is the bar with a few men decked out in golfing gear drinking pints of Foster's. One of the men stands up and begins practicing his putting stroke. His belly hangs over his belt like a large sandbag.

The walls are covered with pennants in glass frames. There must have been twenty or so tables with chairs—the place resembles a three-star restaurant. I go over to the bar.

"How are ye," I say to the tall man in his late sixties garnishing a martini with an olive skewer. His face is burned to a crisp and his double chin is fleshy as he places the drink on a tray.

"What can I do you for?" he responds, not even looking at me.

"I'm supposed to be meeting a fella by the name Lorcan Doyle. Is he around?" The men at the bar glance away when they hear the name.

"I haven't seen him around." He puckers his lips and scratches the bridge of his sunburned nose. "Are you a member?"

"No."

"Then you shouldn't be lingering around here. This is a members club only. You'll be getting me into trouble if you stay here any longer." He leans his gigantic hands on the countertop. The tip of his little finger on his right hand is missing.

"Like I said, I'm meeting this Lorcan fella here before he goes off for his round of golf. Is he down to play today?"

"I can't tell you that."

The man is being a prick so I decide to leave the clubhouse, but not without causing a scene. I head out to the car park. I can feel the old man's eyeballs on me. I see a skinny fella shaped like a stick insect lighting up a cigar with a match. He's standing beside his spanking-new TaylorMade golf clubs.

"You wouldn't have a spare match or two?" I smile. The bloke is wearing a white Nike golf glove and baggy tartan plaid trousers that look like they're from the sixties.

"No problem, my friend." He hands me three.

"You're a good egg," I tell him. "Enjoy your round of golf. It's the perfect day for a low score."

"I wish I could, I've been hitting them in the lake and trees on the front nine."

"There's always a back nine to make it up."

"Emily," he says as an attractive woman around forty rolls a trolley in the car park with her golf bag on top. He walks over to her. I notice he has the trunk of his Tuscan blue Range Rover open. I take a peek inside and see a rain jacket, a five-liter fuel can, and a box of La Gloria Cubana cigars. I don't have much time so I act quickly, grabbing the fuel can.

I leave the car park and walk along the stony wall surrounding the golf course. I can see the lush greens and fairways through the tall trees and bushes. The smell of freshly cut grass is divine. The day is still young, as large broken clouds move effortlessly in the sky. A perfect day for a round of golf or a murder.

A fence about three feet high stands between me and the fields. I throw the fuel can over the other side and step over the fence with great discomfort. The golf course is flat and I keep moving. I really hope the grass isn't damp. I walk across the smooth greens, which feel like carpet on my feet. There's a yellow flagstick that has the number 8 stitched to it on the spotless green. The tricky hole has two large-enough lakes near the front of the green to sink your ball in.

I see a few golfers playing, and I keep my distance, walking through the trees. Not too far from the clubhouse I see a flower bed with the name Milltown Golf Club.

On the tee, on hole number 9, which is a par 3, is a bin. I take a gander inside and see broken tees, split golf balls, Snickers bar wrappers, and ripped-up scorecards. I remove the plastic bag from the garbage bin and begin dumping it all over the flower-bed. I empty all the fuel from the can on it.

The first match blows out instantly. I carefully get the second match going, lighting up a scorecard. It burns quickly. I toss it and watch everything go up in flames like a bonfire. It's like Halloween in the nineties all over again.

I limp out of there fast and head back to the car park, shouting, "Fire! Fire!"

Everybody comes running out of the clubhouse in a panic with pale faces, including the old prick from earlier. With the clubhouse in a frenzy I make my way inside and head over to the computer.

I look out the window and see five golf carts speeding over to the fire, one of them nearly crashing into a bunker. The computer screen has all the bookings for today. I click on the members tab. A list of names shows up. Over three hundred of them. I type in the name Lorcan Doyle.

Two names appear on the screen. I take a photo of the addresses and go back to the main page. I hurry out of the clubhouse before somebody spots me. I look at my phone. The timer on my phone makes my heart ache, reminding me that time is running out for Jack.

CHAPTER NINETEEN

The sky is becoming gloomier, heavier by the second, and the countdown on my phone is losing minutes. It will take me twenty-five minutes to arrive at the first address, located in Blackrock, south of Dublin.

It's been years since I've ventured out to Blackrock, and if I cycle at a good vigorous speed I can probably get there in under twenty minutes. My hip is still sore and there's a temptation to swallow back another chalky pill, but I'm going to wait it out.

My journey begins on Greenfield Park, which takes me through a nice, clean neighborhood to raise a family in. I sometimes dream of living in a nice big house not too far from the city. Olivia and I and possibly a little one running around in the back garden. But that dream feels more distant than ever.

The weight of the revolver inside the fanny pack is bouncing off my thighs as I cycle on Nutley Lane, passing another golf course. The road takes me through St. Vincent's Hospital, where I woke up in a daze after getting hit and flung off my bike.

There's a moment when I see the sunlight shine out from the clouds and Dublin Bay is just magnificent. A sudden gust of wind strikes my face, making my eyes water.

Maretimo Villas. I have arrived. I lock my bike around a parking pole. I check on the time. Five twenty. I hear church bells ringing from down the road. I approach the house with the white gates. I have no time to be messing around.

The plan is to knock on the door, barge my way through, and find Lorcan Doyle, then question him and make sure he's the one

I'm supposed to kill and dump on the Dodder. I've got six hours to complete this job and save poor Jack. They better not hurt him, I swear to God. My body tenses up thinking about it.

I take a deep breath and make my way up to the light-blue decorative Edwardian front door with Celtic-designed stained-glass windows. I slam the tail of the squirrel knocker hard, twice, waiting patiently in a position ready to pounce. The front door swings open. Standing in front of me is an old woman, in her late seventies, possibly early eighties.

She has the friendliest smile planted on her face—it would make your heart melt. Her snow-white hair is short, and she's wearing red cat-eye glasses and an apron with the sleeves rolled up.

"Good evening," she says to me.

"Good evening," I say. "I'm looking for Lorcan Doyle."

"That's my husband, love. He's out back working, come on in." She gestures to me to follow her into the house. "Let me get ye a cuppa. You must be one of his pals. He's gotten to know a lot of people over the years."

"I'm fine for tea."

"Now, don't be like that, I just put the kettle on," she says.

"I know Lorcan from Milltown Golf Club."

"Ah, he loves his golf, can't get him away from it."

The house is spotless clean, smelling of lavender and peaches. She has plants all over the house, in the hallway, the living room, and the kitchen. The fireplaces are on and the house is super cozy. I spot an art deco drinks cabinet made of walnut from the 1930s to my left. That too has plants on top of it.

"You have a lovely home," I say, snooping around the house. There's a painting on the wall near the dinner table. *Young Girl in Front of a Window* by Suzanne Valadon. The painting depicts a girl sitting at a window holding a bouquet of flowers close to her. She ponders out the window. What is she thinking about?

I see black-and-white photos on the mantel of the fireplace. "Is this Lorcan?" I ask, holding the gold picture frame in my hand.

She turns to me. "Yes, that was our wedding day. Can you believe it? We've been married for fifty years." She's now on her knees staring at one of those vintage range cookers with four oven doors. The heat from it makes the kitchen unbearably hot. The kettle goes off.

"So, what did Lorcan do for a living? He isn't much the talker when we play our round of golf."

"He was the CEO of a milk company out in Greystones. He retired a good while ago now." She gets back up off her knees and starts pouring the boiling water into two mugs.

"*The Thinker.*" I walk over to the shelf on the wall, where there is a bronze replica of Auguste Rodin's statue.

"Lorcan made that." She adds milk to the tea. She didn't even ask.

"He really made this?"

"Yes. He picked up sculpting after retiring, that and the golfing, of course."

I look out the back-porch doors. I see a small metal shed painted black. "Can I speak to him?"

"Sure ye can. But don't go for too long, your tea will get cold and I have an apple pie in the oven you can have a bite from."

"I would love that." I smile.

I feel like taking my revolver out of my fanny pack, but something doesn't feel right. It must be the old lady and her kind hospitality. I don't hear a thing out in the back garden except for a dog barking next door. I look at the big tree in the very back of the garden and see why the dog is barking. A large white cat that looks pregnant is lurking in the branches.

I creep up to the shed, pulling on the handle, opening up the door. The hinges squeal, needing a good oiling.

The room is dark and the lights are off. I search the walls, flicking a switch. The shed lights up inside, revealing the many impressive bronze statues on a long table. I recognize some of them. The first one is the Statue of Liberty, followed by the Discus Thrower, then the Christ the Redeemer, as seen in Rio de Janeiro, Brazil. Lorcan for sure has a talent for sculpting.

I look around the shed, but there's no sign of Lorcan Doyle. There's a strong stench of clay inside. This usually happens if it's been exposed too long to air and moisture. I rummage through his workstation, picking up a sculpting tool. I notice something on a small stool to my far right. Sitting on top of the stool is a solid-oak box. A gold rose is engraved on both sides of the box. I get down on my knees and read what it says: **LORCAN, ALWAYS LOVED AND MISSED, IN LOVING MEMORY, REST IN PEACE.**

What in the name of God? Is Lorcan dead? Shit, I have the wrong Lorcan Doyle.

I go back into the house, closing the porch door behind me.

"Hot, hot," shouts the old woman, dropping the tray with the apple pie onto the kitchen table. Her head turns to me. "Who are you?" she says, mystified by my presence. The old woman isn't smiling anymore. She backs away from me.

"I was just here a few moments ago," I say calmly.

"I said who are you?" She grabs a knife from the wooden block on the countertop. It's sharp enough to slice me in half.

I raise my hands in surrender. "I'm here to see your husband, remember?"

Blood rushes to her face. "What have you done to my husband?"

"Calm down. Put the knife down."

"*Where is my husband?*"

"He died, didn't he?"

"No, no, he didn't, he's just working out in his shed. Said he'll be in for supper. I made his favorite, apple pie."

"Put the knife down," I say sternly, the kitchen smelling of sugar and cinnamon. The woman starts crying. Tears are dropping from her wrinkled eyelids. "I'm going to leave now."

I slowly walk backward out into the hallway. She's still gripping the knife, her lips quivering. I don't know what I've got myself into. I leave the house swiftly, avoiding a stabbing from an old woman who has lost her husband.

CHAPTER TWENTY

I climb back on my bike and cycle to the next address, located in Donnybrook. I can't get the vivid image of being in a standoff with an elderly woman and the distinctive smell of apple pie out of my head.

Somehow, I've been involved with too many women holding weapons, ready to fight me, one on one. These Irishwomen are certainly built different, taking no bollocks off anyone, including a scruffy hit man like myself.

I could have unzipped my fanny pack and pulled out my revolver, but the last thing I want is to hurt an innocent old lady and have the neighbors complaining about hearing a gunshot.

Donnybrook is a twenty-minute cycle from Blackrock. I turn right onto Stillorgan Road. To my left is University College Dublin. The bendy road takes me all the way to Donnybrook.

I arrive at the location at six o'clock. My legs are starting to tire out and become sore, particularly my shins. The stinging pain in my hip is infuriating. I pop into a supermarket, leaving the bike outside the entrance to buy a bottle of water with a hint of lime and a peanut butter protein bar.

I get back on my bike, cycling to the address, which is around the corner. I see the house in the distance. It's a big one. I can tell the property has at least five bedrooms and multiple bathrooms.

The peanut butter lingers in my mouth as I sit still on the seat of my bike. I remove a pill from the bottle and plop it in my mouth, swallowing the rest of the water like an absolute savage.

The water dribbles down my neck and onto my shirt, giving me a horrible sensation.

The house is discreetly tucked away on Eglinton Road in a cul de sac. The street is silent, but I do hear the sound of a vacuum blaring out from the house. The front door opens and a woman in her thirties with brown skin, dark-chocolate hair, and rubber gloves appears. She vacuums the doormat with conviction as I approach her. I leave my bike leaning against a wall outside.

"Excuse me," I yell over the sound of the vacuum. She doesn't hear or see me. I lean down with my head tilting to one side like a curious budgie. The woman gets a fright seeing my nosy mug inching toward her. The vacuum suddenly goes off as she snaps her head back.

"Oh, you nearly gave me a heart attack, sir." Her hand is on her chest like she's about to sing the national anthem. She has a thick Latin American accent.

"Sorry to disturb you, but I'm looking for a man by the name of Lorcan Doyle."

"Ah, are you here for the big party?"

"Party?"

"Yes, the commissioner's retirement party. His family are throwing him one this evening."

I'm confused. "Commissioner?"

"Oh, I'm used to calling Mr. Doyle 'commissioner.'"

"I see." And I do, because now I notice the black-and-gold happy-retirement balloons behind her in the kitchen bouncing off the ceiling. "Where is he?"

"He's usually at the pub at this time." The Latin American woman leans her body forward out from the porch, revealing her abalone shell earrings. "His wife, family, and friends are going to surprise him when he comes back."

"I must have got my times mixed up," I say, acting the eejit. "What time is the party starting at?"

"Eight o'clock."

"Which pub is Mr. Doyle at?"

"Arthur Mayne's," she says. "I must get back to work, sir."

"I don't want to get you into trouble, thanks for all your help, love," I say and she gives me a lovely smile.

I've got a couple of hours to kill before I make my move on Lorcan Doyle, but this is going to be a tough one. There's going to be a ton of witnesses and I'll need to find a way to get at him and bring his body to the Dodder.

I take a stroll back on Donnybrook Road, scrolling through the internet on my phone. I search the name *Commissioner Lorcan Doyle*. I click on images. His big head shows up on the screen. The bags under his eyes are heavy, like shopping bags, his mustache identical to Tom Selleck's in *Magnum P.I.*, and his skin pale white like he hasn't seen the sun in years. The photo shows him in his uniform and cap with a somber expression on his face.

I skim through a few articles written up on him. One of the pieces said he had a stroke last year and another said he bought a home in Donnybrook for 1.5 million euro. That's a lot of money for a man like Lorcan. Being a commissioner must bring in the big bucks.

The sky is now dark and the streetlamps have turned on. Across the road is Arthur Mayne's pub, lit up. Through the windows you can see they have hundreds of vintage apothecary bottles, reminding us it used be a chemist.

On the corner is a bookmaker. It's about to close. Two men come wandering out. One of them is pudgy and losing all his hair. The other man, a short fella, is Lorcan Doyle. I watch him leave the bookmaker in a hurry, panicking, with betting slips shaking in his hand.

I see a rough-looking man in a long trench coat and a brown tartan cap with spiderweb tattoos all over his hands. He stops Lorcan by putting his hand on his chest. They get into a heated discussion, which I can't hear clearly. The tattooed man points his index finger close to Lorcan's nose like he's warning him. He then lightly slaps him on the face.

Lorcan keeps walking, entering Arthur Mayne's Pub. I cross the road. The awful taste of the protein bar is still in my mouth. I close the door behind me when I enter the pub. The atmosphere is relaxed and warm. Couples are eating tacos and chicken wings and drinking elaborate cocktails at the front of the pub. I make my way to the back, where it's dark.

I see Lorcan Doyle sitting down in the corner with his headphones in his ears, staring intensely at his phone. I take a seat at the bar on a leather stool. "I'll have a pint of Smithwick's, please," I say to the barwoman, who has curly hair. She reminds me of Olivia. The only difference is that Olivia's hair is fuller and it makes me want to smother my face in it every time I see her.

My phone vibrates in the fanny pack, tickling my belly fat. The text reads *Time is precious. Make sure to take a photo of Lorcan's dead body on the Dodder.*

The headaches are tiptoeing back in like Simone trying to sneak into my bed. The barwoman lands a pint of Ireland's oldest ale in front of me. I pay in cash. I take a big sup of the drink, which goes down wonderfully, and let out a wet cough into my sleeve.

Lorcan Doyle has all his betting slips on the table. The barwoman places a pint of Moretti on his table. I see him shouting at his phone and ripping up his slips in a frenzy, lashing back the pint like it's water.

He never takes off his coat in the two hours I'm waiting at the bar. It's coming up to eight o'clock and Lorcan begins to leave. I finish up my Kilbeggan whiskey on the rocks, scorching my throat. I go for a piss in the toilets, removing the revolver in the stalls, making sure it's loaded. Then I put it back in my fanny pack. It's crunch time.

I leave the pub and walk toward Lorcan's home. There are very few houses around the estate, which is a good sign. The sky is as black as a pint of Guinness, but the stars are out and about twinkling.

There're a few cars parked on the curb outside Lorcan's home. Tonight could smell disaster. So many witnesses, so little time. I must be careful, but in honesty I have no plan. In my line of work, I usual stalk the prey and when the time is right, I attack.

I have four hours to kill Lorcan and drag his body to the river Dodder, which is a short walk from the house. I march along the back-garden wall. It's long, with an old door at the end.

Unfortunately, the wall is too tall to climb and I don't have my lockpick set with me to wiggle my way in. I put on my leather gloves and black COVID-19 face mask, which covers my mouth and nose. I take a few steps back. With all my strength, I use my right foot to kick the door open. I want to scream as the pain in my hip feels like it's been walloped by a baseball.

I quickly walk in, closing the door behind me. The house is even bigger from the back. It has a gigantic glass extension and kitchen where I can see everyone loudly talking and singing to "We Built This City" by Starship. The party has taken off like it's a bleedin' cruise ship.

The sound of a balloon popping startles the guests. They are laughing hysterically as I lurk in the darkness among the trees. To my left is a large garden office with lots of glass. I go inside. I look around and see a couch, desk, and tall cabinet.

The hours are dragging by and I need to make a move soon. The plan is to pull my hood up, cover my mouth with the face mask, and barge into the house, tell everyone to get on the floor, and then I go find Lorcan Doyle and walk him all the way to the Dodder with the gun pointing at him. And when we get to the Dodder, I shoot him dead.

I rub my hands on my face.

That's a stupid fuckin' plan.

Shit! Shit! Shit!

I'm breathing heavily. The night is an utter catastrophe. In the dark, my head is spinning around a hundred miles per hour as I pace back and forth in the garden office.

I hear somebody through the thick glass. I peak outside with my back against the wall. Lorcan is walking out the back of the kitchen. He lights up a cigarette, taking a long drag. I hide in the shadows, peeping out at him. I push the office door ever so slightly to get his attention. I can hear my heartbeat in the quiet room. Leaning against the wall, I remove the loaded revolver from my fanny pack.

I catch a glimpse of him flicking the cigarette into the grass and making his way toward the office. The door opens halfway. He pokes his head in, then pushes the glass door all the way. I grab a handful of his shirt, pull him in, and propel him onto the couch. I quickly shut the door.

"Keep that mouth of yours shut," I order him, pointing the gun. "Commissioner Lorcan Doyle, isn't it?"

"Who are you?" he asks, getting into a more comfortable position.

"Listen up, we don't have much time," I say. "I need to ask you a few questions."

"Did Flanagan send you?"

"Who's he?"

"The one I owe money to."

"How much?" I say.

"Eighty grand."

I make a whistling sound with my lips. "That's a lot of money. The tattoo fella from earlier, was he the bloke you owe money to?"

"He's a nobody... trying to intimidate me."

"Who would want you dead?"

"Do you have all night? Before I was commissioner, I was a chief superintendent, superintendent, inspector, sergeant and Garda officer. I worked my way through the ranks and I'm sure I've pissed off a number of people."

"So, you don't know why somebody sent me to kill you and dump your body on the Dodder?"

"Is that where you going to dump me? Jaysus," he says, eerily calm. "I knew this day would come. I'm not afraid of you."

The timer on my phone is ticking and I wasn't getting a squeak out of Lorcan. He puts his hands on his knees and continues to smile.

I hear something jump on the roof of the office. I look up. Old Lorcan jumps off the couch and comes running at me like a short, demonic boar, slamming me into the wall with all his might, his hand gripping my forearm with the gun. I elbow him in the back hard. He releases a loud groan. I try aiming the aim gun at him, but he has me by the wrist. He throws a punch into my ribs, then my bruised hip. I press my lips tightly together in agony.

He's a strong little fella and he pushes me on top of the desk. Stacks of paper plummet onto the floor and a lamp goes flying. He grinds his false teeth together, putting on a brave display. I throw another elbow, and this time I hit him on the cheekbone. It looks like a sore one. He buckles to his knees. I smack him in the face with the barrel of the gun and he falls on his backside. He puts up a good fight, but now it's time to end this party.

I grab one of the cushions on the couch and place it in front of Lorcan's face, pulling the trigger twice. The shots are loud. I drop the cushion on the floor and see Lorcan lying against the wall, legs apart, with two bullets in his face. Blood splatter all over the wall and his shirt. I've left a mess.

I look around the office. I see the cabinet in the corner. I open it up. Inside are two suitcases. The big one will do. I unzip the suitcase and roll Lorcan's body into it, folding up his legs. I'm glad he's a short fella. I zip the bag up. It's a tight squeeze.

I pull the handle up and start wheeling his body out of the office shed like I'm about to go on vacation. Up above me on the roof is a black cat with amber eyes, peering down at me. The party is still going on in the house. I quickly roll the suitcase out the back door and make my way to Donnybrook Road. The streets are deserted and there's no cars about.

On gray stone in gold lettering it reads: **ANGLESEY BRIDGE 1832**. I rush down some steps, losing control of the suitcase. It falls out of my hands, hitting the bottom and making a splash by the shore. I quickly unzip the suitcase and take a photo of Lorcan in the fetal position like he's a baby in the womb. I send it to Jack's number. I zip the suitcase back up and push it into the river Dodder, watching it float slowly in the cold, murky waters. I remove the revolver from my fanny pack, flinging it into the river, making a splash. I dump the bullets in as well.

The moon is glowing down at me like a torch catching me in the act. I get the chills. What a fuckin' night.

~~KILL LORCAN DOYLE~~

CHAPTER TWENTY-ONE

cycle back home, shattered by tonight's ordeal. I feel like I'm about to collapse and fall off my bike as I enter Smithfield Square, which is now empty and soulless. I wheel my bike into the lobby. Nicholas isn't at the front desk. Instead it's the older woman with the curly caramel hair. She gives me a rigid stare, sipping on her coffee as I enter the elevator.

I get into the loft knackered, knees buckling. I remove my fanny pack like it's a gun belt and throw it on the couch. I use my teeth to pull off my leather gloves, and throw them on the couch, too. I pet Simone on the head and make sure she has food and water in her bowls. I don't have the energy to play with her, so I end up having a quick, warm shower before going straight to bed.

My phone vibrates on the bedside table. Jack's name appears on the screen. The text simply reads: *Job well done. Talk soon.* I try calling Jack's number to see if I can speak to the Bison, but I get no answer. I really hope Jack is okay and they haven't hurt him. My eyelids begin to close. I can feel my body shutting down and darkness looming in on me.

I wake up the next day feeling like I'm hungover, as if I spent all night attempting the Baggot Mile pub crawl. I look at the time on my phone: eleven thirty. I let out a loud sneeze, startling Simone, who is lying down at the end of the bed. I can feel her warm body against my legs. My hip aches. The taste of pale ale lingers in my mouth like a dirty wet sock.

I speedily brush my teeth, floss, and rinse my mouth with minty mouthwash. They say there are about 6 billion bacteria lurking in a human's mouth, so I decide to do an extra thirty seconds of rinsing.

"I need to take you on a walk today, don't I?" I say to the dog staring up at me. I've been neglecting Simone all week. I lean down, sniffing her head. "You also need a shower."

I lift the dog into the shower and hose her down. Still in my fresh undies, I spend the next twenty minutes chasing her around the loft. When she shakes her coat, it drenches the floors. "Ye little shit."

I dry her off with a towel and use a hair dryer to dry her down. She hates it, barking hysterically at it, as if I'm about to tase her. Once she's all dry and clean, I get her on the couch and brush her down. Her coat is now soft and clean.

I put on fresh clothing: black shorts, white T-shirt, and a navy-blue hoodie.

I have to rewash the clothing from the other night, which is still in the washing machine. I give them a whiff. They smell funny. I throw in my clothing from last night for fifteen minutes.

I put on a cup of tea and start cooking two eggs with olive oil. I place two slices of white Brennans bread in the toaster. I wait for it to turn twelve o'clock on my phone, which is charging beside me on the countertop.

I take my vitamins and swallow back the painkiller with a pint of water. The eggs and toast are done. I sprinkle salt and pepper on top and butter up the toast. I finish breakfast in under three minutes.

"Time for your walk," I say to the dog. She jumps off the couch and starts running around vigorously in circles. She guzzles water from the bowl eagerly, nearly knocking it over.

I grab the leash and walk the dog out to the elevator. I stare at my reflection in the mirror. The beard and mustache grow bushier and wilder by the hour.

As I'm leaving, I see a newspaper on top of the coffee table in the lobby. The headline reads "MURDER ON THE DODDER."

I take Simone outside, while the sun is still glimmering and somewhat warm. I do a lap around the square.

I pass the Light House Cinema, where they're showing the extended director's cut of Sergio Leone's *Once Upon a Time in America* and Bob Fosse's *Cabaret*. Simone sniffs a tree, then pees beside it. The river of piss rolls on the path, down the curb, and onto the road.

My phone vibrates in my pocket. Jack's name shows up. I get a tingling sensation in the pit of my stomach.

"Hello," I say.

"Patrick Callen," says the Bison. "Nice touch stuffing Lorcan Doyle in the suitcase. I just read it in the papers this morning. You're sure grabbing all the headlines. The filthy rat was discovered by a ninety-year-old man at Loftus Walk Nursing Home. The old fella was just having his cup of tea when he saw something wash up on the riverbank close to the nursing home. Imagine seeing something like that at his age. You could've given the man a heart attack, Patrick… and killed two people."

"Where's Jack? I did what you asked me to do."

"Don't get hasty, now. I've got another job lined up for ye," he says playfully, like it's all game.

"The deal was to kill Lorcan Doyle and that's it." I grip the leash tightly.

"I never said such a thing." There's a silence for a moment between us. "I sent you something, check your phone." I look down at the text. It's a photo of Jack tied up to a chair with a bloody face. I bite into my bottom lip.

"You better not fuckin' hurt him."

"Then you better do what your told. I'll send you a name and location soon, buddy. You just make sure to keep that bleedin' phone of yours charged."

The Bison hangs up.

"Fuck! Fuck! Fuck!" I grunt to myself, punching my leg. Simone looks up at me with her precious brown eyes, knowing something isn't right.

CHAPTER TWENTY-TWO

Simone runs over to her bowl of water, wagging her tail frantically, when we get back to the loft. I sink my body into the couch, clutching one of the decorative cushions with the red African women printed on them.

The iron mask mounted on the wall looks down at me like it's about to speak to me. Maybe it can give me advice on my next moves.

I hear my phone buzzing in my pocket again. This time it's Caitríona.

"Yeah," I say.

"How did it go with the Sammy Jenkins fella?" She sounds out of breath.

"Who?"

"Don't tell me you haven't done the job yet?"

"Oh, Sammy. Yes. I'll be paying him a visit this afternoon."

"You better, because if you don't, I'm giving the job to somebody else. When you're done with him meet me at the criminal courts later on at five." Caitríona hangs up without saying goodbye.

I pack up my fanny pack with a fully charged mobile phone, sunglasses, leather gloves, keys, headphones, cash, and notebook. I then use a bike pump for my tires. I have a busy day ahead of me. I rub the freshly clean dog one more time on the neck.

"I'll be back later." I kiss the top of her head. The dog licks my cheek. "Ye little devil."

✤   ✤   ✤

Outside my building, I swing my bruised hip over the bike and start pedaling west of the city. It shows twenty-two minutes on the map app on my phone. With my mood being a little low, I plop my headphones into my ears and start playing the only decent song by the band Kiss, "I Was Made for Lovin' You."

Before making a right onto Sarsfield Road, I find myself biking through the Irish National War Memorial Gardens, which pays tribute to the 49,400 Irish soldiers who died in World War I. It's down for a cloudy day, but it's very dark at this time. Now I'm having doubts I'll be returning home dry.

The route takes me uphill on Ballyfermot Road, then onto Kylemore Road. Mostly industrial estates and car dealerships occupy this part of the city. I see a gas station. I cycle over to it, leaving my bike locked outside, and I walk in, removing my headphones.

When I enter, "Bitter Sweet Symphony" by the Verve is playing. I take a stroll down the biscuit aisle. Too many to choose from. Then there's a shelf packed with chocolate Easter eggs. They've gone up in price over the years. These giant eggs go for twenty euro, absolute rip-off.

I pick up a large Smarties Easter egg for three euro. It comes with two tubes of Smarties. Nearly a thousand calories for the thing. Before I leave the gas station, I grab an energy drink from the fridge. I head over to the gym resembling a warehouse, locking my bike outside in the car park.

I end up shoving both tubes of Smarties and the whole chocolate egg down my gob. The Red Bull sugar-free energy drink doesn't mix well with the chocolate in my stomach, but I need a rush before I start throwing shapes and putting my mark on this joker.

I lean back on the bike seat and look up Sammy "The Sleeper" Jenkins on my phone. Five foot nine inches, weighing

155 pounds. Twenty-four years of age with eight wins and zero losses to his name.

He won the lightweight championship with the MMA organization Cage Warriors and recently signed a six-fight deal with the UFC, where he's already won his first two fights, earning him a little over a hundred grand. Not bad for someone who was collecting unemployment benefits three years ago.

His father died when he was young, so the mother took care of him and his four siblings. I use my little finger to get some of the chocolate that's stuck between my bottom teeth. I check his social media. He did a live training-session video five minutes ago in the gym.

Outside the entrance they have a mural of the Colosseum. It's like the scene from the movie *Gladiator* when Russell Crowe stares up and sees the Colosseum for the first time. I can hear the ghost of Oliver Reed whispering in my ear, *"Win the crowd and you will win your freedom."*

I march into the gym and head straight to the front desk, where I'm greeted by a muscular man with arms the size of me legs. Clean-shaven, dark hair freshly trimmed, fake tan on his arms, hands, and face as if he just competed in a bodybuilding show recently. The veins pop out as he shakes his bottle with vanilla protein inside.

I lean against the countertop. "I'm looking for a day pass."

"We can do that or we can give you a discount if you sign up right now for a twelve-month membership," he replies, putting his revolting shake down beside my hand. "It's a good deal. You get the first month free." His porcelain veneer smile makes me feel uncomfortable.

"I'm okay, it's just for today," I say.

"Your call," he says. "It will be fifteen euro."

"Fifteen euro for a one-day pass, Jaysus," I groan like an old granny, even though I did just spend six euro on a Smarties Easter egg and energy drink.

"Yep."

"Do I get a massage with that?"

"Nope, just access to the gym, locker rooms, showers, and this." He hands me a white towel.

"Fantastic." I snatch the towel from his paws. The towel has his fake-tanned fingertip markings all over it like poop stains. I hand the juicehead his fifteen euro.

The gym is a big one. All the equipment is in red and black with rough-looking faces working out on it. I stare up at the wall in front of me. The man himself, Arnold Schwarzenegger, in black and white. Arms wide open like a wandering albatross. His tiny waist, ripped six-pack, and bulging arms are on display along with his infamous smile showing the slight gap in his front teeth. I remember years ago watching Arnold in the documentary *Pumping Iron*, which was all about the golden era of body-building in the 1970s.

I pace around the gym I have no business in with the stained towel over my shoulder. "Take Me to Church" by Hozier comes on loudly, piercing my ears.

Where is this little prick?

Beside the cardio machines there's a boxing ring. A young one with dark hair in a ponytail is kicking pads. She grunts every time she kicks the pad high above the guy's head, nearly knocking him over. She leans over the ropes, out of breath, spitting her gum shield out of her mouth. Our eyes meet for a second.

I keep moving. To my right, I see mats and an octagon cage. I peak through the metallic wired fence and see the face of Sammy "The Sleeper" Jenkins. His buzz-cut hairstyle like Liam Gallagher from Oasis. Hollow eyes. Skin white as milk, paper-thin from cutting weight. His muscles in great detail like a Michelangelo sketch. Blood is pumping through his veins, which are protruding from his skin. He rolls around the octagon with another fighter in red shorts, his feet leaving wet footprints on the mat.

I watch until he finishes up. His coach squirts water into his mouth from a bottle. He starts walking out of the octagon, his four-ounce gloves still on.

"Sammy," I say as he walks away. He doesn't hear me. "Sammy," I say again, this time louder, over Hozier singing the chorus. He turns around. I give him a nod to come over.

"I'm not speaking to any press. I've done all my interviews yesterday."

"I'm not with the press. I just want to have a chat."

He struts over to me sticking his gum shield down the front of his shorts. "About what?"

"I've been hearing you've been causing a stir around the city. Drop-kicking people at nightclubs, running another over with your car, and choking a sixty-year-old man out, putting him in the hospital."

"What of it? Are you the bloody Garda?"

"Worse than that," I say.

"What's your end game, ol' fella? You should leave, mate, or I might have to drop-kick you in the chin… maybe knock that stupid mustache off your face." He grins with a mouthful of sharp teeth like Jaws.

"Stop fucking around, you hear me? I don't want to see you again because the next time I do, I'll have to—"

"You have to what?" He pokes his finger hard on my left pec. "I will fuckin' bury you, old man."

"Fuckin' do it." I get close to his face. I feel my nostrils flicker. His coach comes over to join the party. Tall skinny fella with a landing-strip goatee and a conch piercing on his right ear.

"What's goin' on here?" he asks.

"This fella wants to spar," Sammy says to him.

"You have a fight in two weeks. There's no need to be messin' around now," the coach says.

"You should listen to your coach," I sneer.

"In the octagon now," he shouts at me, his warm breath blowing on my face. His coach's lips are tightening up. He's pissed off with the situation about to occur.

"You better not get injured." The coach folds his arms.

Sammy runs up the steps into the octagon. I follow him.

"Look at this ol' fella wearing slippers and a fanny pack. Are you fuckin' kidding me?" He lobs me a pair of MMA gloves, which are so thin that I might as well be bare-knuckling. I remove my hoodie and slippers, placing them on the side with my fanny pack.

He starts bouncing on his feet, hands up, ready to go. "Three two-minute rounds," he bellows, plopping the gum shield back into his mouth. "I'll try to put you away early."

His trainer presses a button on a timer. The red digits begin to go down. "Come on, then, throw us your best shot, Mr. Monopoly." Jaysus, I'm not that feckin' old. A small crowd gathers around the cage.

I jab my right hand at him. He moves to the side. I strike again with the left, feeling the pain in my hip. He ducks. "Too slow," he says, quickly circling me, showboating. He flings a kick at my left thigh. I check it. It stings me like a motherfucker. The throbbing trickles up to my bruised hip.

He throws a right hand, then a left, hitting me on the side of the head, but I manage to move backward to soften the blows. I glance at the clock. Ten seconds left and I'm out of breath, out of fuckin' shape. He throws a side kick, striking me dead on the ribs. I fall on one knee, winded. The buzzer on the timer goes off, sounding like a heart monitor when somebody dies. "Lucky bastard," he says.

Second round. I move about the cage trying to limber myself up. I lunge at him with a punch, hitting him clean in the jaw. He doesn't move too far. The psychotic smile on his face is like the Joker. He spits some blood out on the canvas. One minute on the clock. He hits me with a brutal calf kick, then throws a combination to my head, connecting an uppercut to my jaw. My beard doesn't act as a cushion, which I'd hoped for.

I feel dizzy and taste a mix of blood, chocolate, and the tangy Red Bull in my mouth. He comes running at me again, picking me up, then violently throwing me on my back. "Come on, fight back," he cackles, lying on top of me, his forearm against my neck. He slaps me in the face and digs his knee into my chest. I find it hard to breathe.

"Ten seconds," yells the coach.

I hold out and make it through the round. I'm knackered. My legs wobble like the perfect panna cotta. I take in a deep breath when I get up off the canvas. My body feels heavy, tight.

Sammy looks like a man who could do another twenty rounds. I wipe my face with the towel. I have a sneaky suspicion the fake tan is on my forehead.

The third round. I can make it through this. I put my tired fists up. This is my moment to shine. To knock the smug expression off his face. He comes at me. I throw a punch as hard as I can. He ducks. And tackles me to the ground. He puts all his weight on me, throwing a few vicious punches. I block with my arms.

Then he rolls me over, getting me in a guillotine, clamping onto my neck. I can feel the blood fill my face like a poured glass of red wine. I try to slip my head out but I can't. He has me locked in. My eyes are closing and I can't breathe.

"Stop! Stop!" I hear someone shout. As I'm about to pass out, his arm releases. I roll over flat on my back on the canvas like I'm doing a snow angel.

"You're a lucky man," Sammy says standing over me. My vision is off. "The Sleeper nearly got you. Next time my coach won't be here to save your arse. I don't want to see your face around here again, you got that? You and your fanny pack," he says, throwing it at me.

I can't respond. I'm beat. I was five seconds away from never waking up again. I can see my stomach go up and down like a trampoline.

I drag myself out of the gym for fresh air. My body beat-up in the car park. I remove my notebook from my fanny pack and put a shaky line through my to-do list. It didn't feel so nice.

SAMMY "THE SLEEPER" JENKINS

CHAPTER TWENTY-THREE

What a fuckin' disaster. I cycle back into town with sore ribs, chest pain, and my neck feeling like a snake has been wrapped around it. I did get a few digs in, but nothing to brag about at the local pub.

It's a loss on my record. I should have known better than to be fighting on his turf. I should have just threatened the little prick with a gun at his home. Maybe put a sharp knife to his mother's throat or threatened to drown one of his nieces in the bathtub. Too far? It would have scared the little rat.

I should've left my ego at the door. I'm not in the mood to shovel a big meal down my gullet right now. My intestines hurt from the combination of kicks and junk food I ate earlier.

They say treat your body like a temple. I was a few seconds away from going night-night and I was another five minutes away from defecating myself.

A tiny raindrop falls from the sky and lands on my forehead like a leak from a dodgy pipe as I pedal a little faster in the bike lane. My calf muscles are tender and my ears are on fire. I glance at the cracked mirror on my handlebar. My ears are scorching red. Sammy roughed me up good, the bastard.

Dame Street is dreadful. This time last month it was even worse—nearly half a million people were on the streets celebrating St. Patrick's Day. Marching bands from around the world, tourists wearing bright green hats waving Irish flags in one hand and holding a pint of Guinness in the other.

The traffic is a joke as I weave my way around a taxi turning right, finding myself on Suffolk Street passing the Molly Malone statue. The woman who sold fish during the day and her body at night. She pushes a cart with baskets of fish, cockles, and mussels, her bronze breasts almost spilling out from her low-cut top.

I cycle on Nassau Street and turn into Merrion Square Park. I get off my bike and roll it inside. To my left, resting on a thirty-ton white quartz boulder, is the statue of Oscar Wilde, his jacket made of green nephrite jade and his collars and cuffs of thulite. A walking tour stands around the statue taking photos.

Not far from the flamboyant statue of Wilde is a playground where kids are running about and screaming hysterically, like they have eaten too many sugary sweets.

I continue rolling my bike through the quaint park, passing a throne they call the Joker's Chair dedicated to Dermot Morgan, who starred in the ever-popular TV sitcom *Father Ted*. I sit on the throne, leaving my bike on the grass, which resembles soft waves.

Something is bugging me. I stare at the robin singing on the bald bust next to me. Now I'm like *The Thinker*. Lorcan Doyle said the name Flanagan before I murdered him. I scroll through my contacts on my phone and come across the initials JJ. I call the number.

"Hello," I say.

"Patrick, what's the story, bud?" Junkie Jake says in his thick inner-city accent.

"I need your help."

"What kind of help?"

"Do you know any sharks in the city by the name of Flanagan?" I ask.

"Flanagan… let me think. Flanagan, Flanagan. Yes, I actually do." There's a silence on the phone.

"Go ahead, then."

"I can give you a location for fifty quid."

"Would you fuckin' stop it. How many times have I overpaid you for information over the years?"

"I think I'm very fair with my prices," JJ says.

"I'll fix you up later, then."

"Okay. There's a bloke by the name Neil Flanagan who lives in Temple Bar with his brother."

"Does his brother have tattoos all over his hands?"

"Yeah, how did ye know that?" JJ says. "They're low-level scumbags, to be honest. They target old people, students, and bookmakers all over town, loaning out thousands with stupid amounts of interest."

I sneeze into my sleeve. "Did you hear about the murder on the Dodder?"

"Yeah, it was all over the news. He was a shady bastard, that commissioner."

"In what way?"

"I remember him arresting a cousin of mine back in the day," he says. "He planted five grams of cocaine on him and then he tried to make him rat on his mates. A right prick he was. He's in a better place now, six feet under, ha!"

"Who do you think would want him dead?"

"Too many to count from, but I have a gut feeling he pissed off some big guns."

"How's that?" I ask.

"Shot twice in the head and then dumped in the river inside a bleedin' suitcase. That's psychotic, if ye ask me. The people who ordered the hit wanted to send a fuckin' message."

"So, this Neil fella lives in Temple Bar?"

"Yeah, right above the Queen of Tarts café."

"I'll be around to you this week sometime," I say.

"Sounds good, pal, just give us a heads-up beforehand."

A couple in their fifties are standing in front of me with fanny packs similar to mine around their waists and shirts tucked away into their trousers. They look German or Dutch, who fuckin' knows. They start taking photos of me like I'm part of the throne.

I get my arse off the bronze throne and make my way over to the picnic tables to the far side of the park. I stare at the time. Quarter to four. I'm early. I sit down on the bench feeling nervous.

I turn my head and the love of my life is standing a few feet away from me. Olivia's curls are blowing against her face as a stormy wind tries to scoop us away. I immediately stand up. She has her hands in the pockets of her rain jacket.

"Olivia," I say as she steps closer to me. I don't know if I should kiss her on the cheek or give her the gentlest of hugs. The moment becomes awkward between us. She has a veil of sadness across her face and a tiredness like she hasn't slept for days. We both plant ourselves down on the bench, keeping our distance, as if I have a virus.

"What happened to you?" she says.

I touch my forehead. "It's just a scratch."

"It's always just a scratch with you. When are you going to stop lying to me?"

I take a deep breath, but I don't know what to say. My mouth is dry. I can only look into her sad eyes.

"I've had enough playing games, Patrick. It's like living with a stranger. I talked to Nocturnal. He said you did a job for him a few days ago. Is this true?"

My body feels numb. "I did, but I was going to tell y—"

"I knew it." She stands up, furious. "You lied to me."

"What else did he tell you?"

"He said you paid him off so I wouldn't have to work for him again."

"Isn't that a good thing? I did it so you wouldn't get hurt anymore and we could be together."

She looks down at me in judgment. "What do you *really* do for a living, Patrick? And don't tell me you work in a fuckin' bike shop. Are you a drug dealer?"

"No!"

"A bagman?"

"No!"

"A robber?"

"No!'

"A killer?"

"Yes!" I shout, feeling something snap in me. "I kill pedos, rapists, and other lowlifes, and I get paid for it. Is that what you wanted to hear? Happy now?"

Olivia's face goes pale. She knows I am telling the truth. She's shocked. So am I. I'm speechless as the wind picks up even more, fiercely blowing her curls.

"You *kill* people for money? Jesus Christ, I can't believe this!" Olivia shakes her head, totally flustered, and turns her back to me. "I need to go."

She rushes away. I try standing up too quickly and my hip gives out. All I can do is watch her go.

~~MERRION SQUARE PARK~~

CHAPTER TWENTY-FOUR

I watch Olivia practically run out of the park. My heart is broken again. The rain comes spiraling down from the gray sky. I pull my hood over my wet hair and pick up my bike from the grass and begin cycling out of Merrion Square, saddened.

Too many thoughts are rushing through my head. I've just told Olivia I'm a killer. I've never said those words out loud.

There's nothing I want to do more than get back with Olivia, and now that the truth has come out, I wonder if I will ever see her again.

Then I think of Jack. I've lost Olivia and I cannot lose Jack. I can't let him die in the hands of some lunatic. I have to save him.

I cycle over to the Ginger Man pub on Fenian Street to take shelter. I stand outside, watching the rain flood the roads and paths.

The pub is empty when I poke my head in.

"Miserable day," says the barman. He is in his sixties, with a thin mustache.

"Do you have anything hot to drink?"

"I can make you a cuppa tea," he says.

"That would be nice, with some milk and a sweetener."

"Coming right up." The old fella goes back inside singing the lyrics to "Red Is the Rose." I try paying the old fella at the bar for the cup of tea, but he refuses.

With warm tea inside me belly, I get back on me bike and head to my next destination, which is fifteen minutes away. The rain subsides to a measly dribble like the last few drops of water coming out of a garden nozzle.

The trip takes me back to the quays, with a view of the Liffey to my right. I pass the Millennium Bridge, which is lit up in different colors like a rainbow. The traffic is nasty on the quays as I make a hard right over the Frank Sherwin Bridge. The magnificent Guinness brewery is across the dirty Liffey. I forget how enormous the place is.

I lock my bike outside the Soldiers' Institute, founded in 1880, on Conyngham Road. Now the splendid Victorian building serves as a shelter for the homeless.

I skip across the road, avoiding getting hit by a road sweeper van. I walk into a modern building with lots of glass. Inside, barristers run about, late for their court appearances. As the glass elevator ascends, I can see all the ceiling pot lights illuminate. I receive a text from Caitríona. *Room number 3. Ground floor.*

I see the room on the far side of the building. Inside are wooden benches like pews in a church, an empty jury box, four monitors mounted on walls, and bright red carpet on the floors, as if it's a Hollywood awards event.

"Over here, fool," Caitríona whispers to my right. She's suited and booted in all black. I sit down and slide across to her.

"What are we doing here?" I ask.

"I like to watch the court cases live in the flesh," she replies, eating the last piece of her orange. The leftover peel sits between us, leaving the distinctive citrus scent mingling in the room like an air freshener.

A judge enters the court, wearing a black gown, a waistcoat, a frock coat, and a white band around his neck. He has gray hair lodged on the top of his head, but it's thin, similar to a bird's nest I saw in St. Stephen's Green the other day.

"I heard you had your hands full with Sammy 'The Sleeper' Jenkins."

"How so?" I see the two bulky security men at the far left of the courtroom. There's also a woman in her thirties sitting down beside a man in a suit. Probably her solicitor.

Caitríona nudges me with her elbow. I look down as she shows me her phone. She plays a video titled *Old man gets slept*. The volume is high. All I see is a blurry video of Sammy strangling the life out of me in an octagon cage. For fuck's sake.

The judge makes an *ahem* sound as he sits down in his leather chair. Caitríona puts her phone away.

"Jesus Christ," I say, "who sent you that?"

"It's all over the internet. I found it funny at first, but then the client calls me this morning saying, why isn't Sammy's beaten-up face all over the news?"

"You weren't there. I got a few punches in." We all stand up in the courtroom. Caitríona is still chewing on the piece of orange.

"Admit it, you lost the fight. Why didn't you threaten the little cunt with a gun or knife?" she asks.

"I know, I know." We sit back down. "It didn't go as planned."

"You could say that again. The woman isn't paying the rest until he's hurt bad and humiliated." To the far left, a rough-looking man enters the courtroom handcuffed. His head is shaved and faded tattoos cover his arms. His skin and eyes are pale yellow like he has a case of jaundice. "I won't tell the Bronze Man. Did you hear what happened?"

"No."

"The roof of the bar caved in last night. The place got flooded, damaging some of the electricals and flooring."

"Jaysus."

"You should see the hole in the ceiling. I feel bad for her, she's put a lot of money into that bar. You should pay a visit, she's there all evening." Caitríona removes a tissue from her pocket and spits the pip into it. "It's another reason why I'm here."

"The court find no words to describe these heinous crimes you have done against your two children…," the judge says, staring down into the man's sickly eyes.

"What's going on here?" I ask.

"Be quiet, will ye?"

"You will serve six months in prison," the judge says sternly. The woman to the left lets out a whimpering cry, which ricochets off the courtroom walls.

"Is that all!" Caitríona yells. "Absolute joke!"

"Silence!" the judge shrieks, almost losing his voice.

"Dirtbird!" yells an older woman sitting in the front row. She looks like the young woman's mother. "Lock him up for good!"

"What's going on?" I am so confused. The judge leaves the courtroom as everyone stands up.

"This is my chance to shine," Caitríona says.

A young woman is crying hysterically as the bloke is dragged away by security. She lays her head in the arms of her mother, upset. They start walking out of the courtroom. Caitríona stands in front of the two. I sit and watch.

"Here." Caitríona presents them with a card between her fingertips. "I'm sorry to hear what happened to your kids. Call me if you want him sorted out in six months' time. I can give you a good price." They don't respond. The young woman thinks about it. Her red eyes look sore and her sternum is protruding from her skin.

She reaches out her frail hand, taking the card from Caitríona's fingertips. The young one wipes her tears with the sleeve of her denim jacket, holding the card to her chest, nodding.

We both stand outside the courthouse. The last of today's glorious sunlight is beaming down on us, as if summer wants to come sooner. The dirty clouds have vanished and gone east.

"So, this is what you're doing hanging around the court-house." I plop my sunglasses on.

"I have to get the clients somehow, don't I?" she responds.

"I suppose."

We walk over to the main road. "That scumbag inside got six months in prison for sexually abusing his two children. The world is gone mental. I'm heading to the district court now and then I'm off to Leeson Street."

"What's on Leeson Street?"

"The rape crisis center." She presses her car key remote. A black-and-white Smart Forfour coupe flashes. "I might catch a few pissed-off victims who need a job done," she adds in as we walk over to her tiny car. She opens the door and steps inside. The car shakes. "Sort that imbecile Sammy out this week. I don't want unhappy clients on my watch. If you don't sort it out, I'll get someone who can."

"I'll have it sorted, trust me."

She starts the car. "The last fella who said *trust me*, I found him dead with three bullets in his back in a swimming pool." I see the dog in the back seat still wearing the cone. "I would give you a lift but your bike doesn't have a chance of fitting in here."

"It's fine."

"I'll keep you posted if I have any more jobs for ye. If you don't hear from me soon, we'll all be signing on the bleedin' unemployment." She slams the door shut and drives off. My skin feels dry and itchy. I reach into my fanny pack and remove my notebook, crossing off me to-do list.

THE CRIMINAL COURTS OF JUSTICE

CHAPTER TWENTY-FIVE

I swallow back a pill and stare up at the sky. It's gone dark and gloomy. I get back on my bike and cycle toward Temple Bar.

After-work drinks and dinners are popular on these streets. The cobblestone pedestrian lanes in Temple Bar are hazardous as usual. If I clip one of these stones wrong, it's good night. But it might not be the stones that will have me flying over the handlebars flat on my face—it might be the hundreds of visitors. The news said almost 6.6 million passengers have traveled through Dublin Airport in the last four months. My arms wobble fitfully as I grip the handlebars on slippery Essex Street.

I make it to Cow's Lane, where the paths are smooth, and to my right is the back way into Smock Alley Theatre, converted from a nineteenth-century church building.

The Queen of Tarts café is dark red with awards plaques on the wall near the entrance and bistro tables and chairs outside. The café is closed and the lane is silent, which feels strange because a couple of streets over its hectic, with traditional Irish music playing and tourists drinking the most expensive pints in Dublin.

I lock my bike on the handrail of a wheelchair ramp outside a bookshop. The collected poems by Seamus Heaney is on display in the shop window.

I wander into the main entrance of the apartment building next to the café and go inside. There're about ten letter boxes on the wall and nobody is at the front desk. There's a bouquet of lavender and pink roses on the countertop.

I press the elevator call button on the wall and wait for the car to descend. It rumbles beyond the walls. The doors slide open. A short fella wearing a New England Patriots cap exits. I recognize the logo from the Tom Brady years.

I enter the elevator and I press the number 1 button. The building only has four floors. The doors reopen. I exit the elevator. To my right the streetlamp is turning on, shining through the high glass window in the hallway. I reach into my fanny pack, remove a face mask, and put it on.

I give the door a hard knock. The door opens up. It's the same fella I saw outside at the bookmaker talking to Lorcan Doyle. The one with spiderweb tattoos all over his hands.

"I'm looking for Neil Flanagan," I say to him.

"Who are you?"

"Are you listening? I'm looking for Neil Flanagan."

"I don't know who the fuck you think you are showing up at my doorstep asking for Neil in that tone." He edges closer to me. I have no time for this clown so I punch him right on the top of his nose.

"Get the fuck in there," I drag him into the living room, throwing him on the floor. Some blood drips from his nose onto the floor. I see a cricket bat leaning against the wall near the kitchen. I pick it up and run over to the large plasma TV and start smashing it to pieces.

"Hey! Not the fuckin' TV," he yells, coming toward me. I hit him again, this time with the toe part of the cricket bat, knocking him back on the couch.

"Sit down, now," I say.

"Jesus Christ... who the fuck are you?" There's blood on his white T-shirt.

"Listen up, dirtbird. I need to know who wanted Lorcan Doyle dead."

"Who?"

"The commissioner," I shout back at him.

"That old fool. Do you think I'm responsible for that?" I hear a noise coming from the bathroom. I press my index finger to my lips to shut the scumbag up. I creep over to the bathroom door. I quickly turn the doorknob and open it up. A man with a towel around his waist comes running out, trying to attack me. I smack him in the stomach and he falls down on his knees.

"You must be Neil. Go join your runt of a brother on the couch." I smack him on the backside with the cricket bat.

The bloke is still wet and has a massive tattoo of a lion's head covering his whole back. He's heavier than his brother and has stretch marks on his hips. I lean my back against the window overlooking the café. "Now, fill me in on why you had Lorcan Doyle murdered."

"We didn't do that shit. Are you mad?" Neil holds his bloated stomach.

"But aren't you two the big tough guys who lend out money to oldies and threaten them if they don't pay up?"

"There's a difference in threatening someone and killing them," Neil says. "These people we loan out to always pay up. Unless they go killing themselves. Then we threaten the families."

"Oh, aren't you two just fine men," I say.

"Here, everyone has to make a living. Lorcan Doyle wasn't no sweetheart. He had a gambling issue and worked with shady people."

"Fucker still owes us money even if he's dead," the other one says. "The wife will have to pay up."

"So, now that we've established that Lorcan was no angel, who do you think ordered the hit?"

"Who bleedin' knows." Neil's hair is dripping on the floor. "Like I said, he worked with shady people."

"Which ones?"

"All I know is that he used to run the port."

"What do you mean?"

"He would pass containers coming into Dublin with contraband inside them," Neil says.

"How do you know all this?"

"A friend of mine worked down there at the customs."

"Where is this friend of yours now?"

"Dead. Found in his home with a heroine needle sticking out from his arm. He never touched a drug in his life," Neil says.

"You think the commissioner had something to do with it?" I ask. Neil nods. "Why didn't he have you killed?"

"We've never had any problems with the commissioner. He always paid up on time. He loves to gamble too much. Well, he used to."

I say, "That's all you know?"

"I swear."

"You better buy us a new TV," the other one says to me, blood smudged all over his chin and down his neck.

I chuckle slightly to myself, leaving the flat with the cricket bat.

On the way back home I drop into Lidl supermarket on Thomas Street, lugging the cricket bat around with me. It has bloodstains on it. I get back to the loft exhausted, my hip still tender. All this running around cannot be doing me any good if I want to heal quickly.

I drop the bag of food on the kitchen countertop and give Simone a good petting down. I leave the cricket bat against the wall.

I down a pint of water, then begin cooking. I start with chopping up garlic cloves and ginger before throwing it all into a pot, adding chicken stock, soy sauce, Worcestershire sauce, chili powder, and white sugar. Next, I add water and wait for it to come to a boil before reducing the heat and letting it simmer for five minutes.

Ramen noodles are boiling in another pot and so are my eggs in a smaller one. I drain the noodles and set them aside. In a frying pan, I start cooking sliced chicken with sesame oil. I strain the stock into a fresh pan and begin boiling it.

I plop my noodles in a bowl with the cooked chicken. I add spinach, sliced green spring onions, and sweet corn to the bowl along with my stock. It smells delicious. Finally, I sprinkle sesame seeds over the meal. I grab a pair of chopsticks from the drawer. The messy kitchen is giving anxiety.

It doesn't take me too long to devour the food. I give Simone some of the chicken. She loves it.

My phone vibrates loudly on the coffee table. I get up off the stool and pick it up. The name Jack appears on the screen. I answer the call.

"Hello," I say.

"Patrick, me auld flower," the Bison says joyfully. "I need you to do a small job for me. It shouldn't be too difficult for a professional like yourself."

"I want to talk to Jack," I say. "I'm done playing games."

"The game isn't over just yet, Patrick. But since ye did a good job on Lorcan, I'll let you speak to your buddy Jack."

"Patrick, can ye hear me?" I hear Jack's voice say. "You don't have to do this… you don't have to kill for him."

"Jack!"

"That's all you get, Patrick," the Bison says in a more serious tone. "Now, get a pen and paper, you need to listen carefully." I run up the stairs, the dog follows, and I grab a pen from me beside table. "Dylan McCarthy. He'll be attending the Shelbourne races tomorrow at seven o'clock. I want Mr. Handsome dead and dumped in the Dodder by midnight," he says as I write on the white walls in the bedroom like a mad mathematician trying to solve an equation. "Did you get all that?"

"Yes," I respond, out of breath.

"Talk soon." The phone hangs up.

I slowly bring my sore body back downstairs. I tie my hair up into a man bun and start cleaning the chaos in the kitchen. Afterward, I vacuum, wash the floors, and put my dry clothing away.

I go back upstairs with my notebook in my hand and lie on the bed. I start writing up a to-do list. The name Dylan McCarthy is scribbled on the wall above my head. I recognize the name.

A text message flashes up on my phone. The name Nocturnal pops up, sending a shooting pain down in my hip. The message simply reads *Trinity College Library, eight o'clock.* Simone is sitting down in front of me with her tongue out, flapping her tail excitedly. She lets out a moan while using her paw to scrape at my toes.

"Simone, don't be bold, now," I say to her. She replies with a bark followed by a growl. "Why are you like this?"

TO-DO LIST

THE BRONZE MAN

TRINITY COLLEGE LIBRARY

GUN II

JUNKIE JAKE

THE SHELBOURNE RACETRACK

CHAPTER TWENTY-SIX

Simone pulls me along the quays over Mellows Bridge, Dublin's oldest bridge. It's like I'm water-skiing on the paths. The stars are glittering away in the black sky on a cold evening.

I cross the road, passing the Brazen Head pub, established in 1198, making it Ireland's oldest pub. Visitors are taking photos outside in front of the place.

St. Audoen's Church is to my left. The dog is buzzing with energy as we walk on a narrow street close to Dublin Castle. St. Stephen's Green is closed, which saddens Simone as she pokes her head through the railings, sniffing the greenery. She knows the swans, ducks, and pigeons are beyond the gates.

The paths are greasy from the rain earlier as I make it on Baggot Street. I see the Bronze Man's security man outside the Crazy Owl breathing in the fresh air with his hands in his coat pockets. His long hair is down to his shoulders, like an immaculate mane on a horse.

"Evening, Slim," I say to him. The dog sniffs his shiny shoes. Then she licks his leg. "She likes you." Slim doesn't respond and instead gives me a hard stare.

The floors are wet when I enter the bar. It's opaque and cold. "Jesus, what happened here? Did ye get hit by an asteroid?" I say, staring up at the massive hole in the ceiling. It must be ten feet wide.

The Bronze Man is sitting at the bar. She takes a long drag from her Juan Lopez cigar. She blows out the thick smoke from her mouth like she's whistling. A cool breeze enters the Crazy Owl, swallowing up the smoke.

"Don't you start," she replies, turning around on the stool. "The roofer was by earlier."

"What did he say?"

"Around forty grand to repair the roof."

"Fuckin' hell."

"That's not including floor and electrical damage." She sips on a glass of whiskey.

When I get closer, it looks like she's already a few deep. I let the dog off her leash to walk about, and I sit beside her at the bar.

"Sounds like a right nightmare, if you ask me."

"You should've seen opening night. The place was packed wall to wall…the reviews were spectacular." She takes another long drag from the cigar before spewing the smoke out from her lips. "The *Times* said the Crazy Owl has a classy atmosphere with snazzy cocktails and the best live band in the city. Will surely be in the running for bar of the year… can ye believe it?"

"Here, you're acting like it's all over. I'm sure you can fix this. You know I don't like using sporting analogies, but there's two halves in a football match and you're just taking a water break."

"Don't mind the feckin' match. I'm in the relegation zone and my team is about to go bust." She puts the cigar into an ashtray. "I already put a fortune into it. I'm not sure I can keep the lights on any longer."

There's a daunting silence between us. I can hear a dripping sound coming from the ceiling. Simone rubs her big head against my bare leg, which tickles me. "Did ye hear about that murder on the Dodder? Some joker named Lorcan Doyle found shot dead and stuffed in a suitcase."

"Oh, yeah." The Bronze Man takes another swig of her whiskey. She pours more Redbreast into her glass, spilling some of it on the counter. "You want some? It's the good stuff."

"I'm grand. Heard he was a commissioner," I say.

"Yeah, a dirty scoundrel of man he was," she replies with a crooked smile.

"How so?"

"Wasn't he caught cheating on his wife with a skanky hooker? No offence. Olivia wasn't skanky... she was a beautiful escort. How is Olivia doing?"

"We're taking a break," I say. My shoulders slump forward.

"How sad. I keep telling you this." She leans closer to me. "You can't be Mr. Assassin and Prince Charming at the same time. Ye feckin' eejit."

"This Lorcan fella was in it deep?"

"Yeah, I reckon he was involved with some big heads."

"Like the McCarthys?"

She glances at me. "What made you say that?"

"I heard he worked on the ports and the McCarthys are the biggest gang in Dublin at the moment, I suppose."

"They're dangerous people, those McCarthys. Stay clear of them."

"Do you think they had any involvement with the killing of Lorcan Doyle?"

"Why are you asking me all these questions? Lorcan Doyle this... McCarthys that. Enough already."

The Bronze Man is getting too drunk for me to be fishing for information. Her breath stinks of cigars and whiskey.

"I'm going to head," I say.

"Caitríona told me you had trouble with the MMA fighter. I hope work isn't getting too hectic for ye."

THE BRONZE MAN

CHAPTER TWENTY-SEVEN

It wasn't the time or place to be spilling my guts out to the Bronze Man about the kidnapping of Jack Magee and how I murdered Lorcan Doyle. She really wasn't in the right state of mind to talk, and the minute I mentioned the McCarthys, she got all touchy.

Before my next meeting, I pop into a café next door to a sweater shop on Nassau Street. I order a small latte, adding brown sugar to it. The slice of red velvet cake behind the thick glass is tempting, but my eating window closes soon. Plus, I'm feeling a little chunky after the ramen noodles from earlier.

The dog sits down beside me, her tongue still hanging out of her mouth. She's delighted to be outdoors and not trapped in the stuffy loft all day. I open up the browser on my phone, typing the words *Dylan McCarthy aka Mr. Handsome, son of Thomas McCarthy, Irelands biggest drug lord*. Well, that's just fantastic.

I read the first article on him, which says he's visiting Dublin for the weekend from Spain for a friend's birthday party. Apparently, he's not involved with his dad's drug operation, which has been going since the late nineties.

I see why he got the name Mr. Handsome. The bloke looks like something out of a Dolce & Gabbana commercial. Blond hair, strong jawline, and the perfect size nose. He owns a couple of restaurants in Málaga and a pub in Sevilla.

The papers have tabs on all the McCarthys and seem to know their every move. I'm certain Dylan won't be easy to get my hands on. I glance at the time. Nearly eight o'clock. I dump the rest of my latte in the bin. It's starting to give me an upset stomach. I regret not ordering the peppermint tea instead.

We walk at a good pace to College Green and hear the screeching sound of the tram coming around the bend like a slow worm. We arrive at the main entrance to Trinity College. The campus is peaceful at this time and looks to be closing up. Trinity was founded in 1592 by Queen Elizabeth I, making it Ireland's oldest university, its architecture similar to the University of Oxford's, with its vast gray walls. Truly a fine campus. The front gate is made of oak with a French polish. It wasn't too long ago that a driver rammed his car through the front gate, destroying it. It was repaired in a matter of days.

The copper-bronze statue of novelist, playwright, and poet Oliver Goldsmith gazes down at me with a playful pose. He has a pen poised in one hand and is reading a book in the other. His tailcoat is dripping in dry bird poop. I walk quickly inside with the dog.

Parliament Square sits in silence, with figurative keystones depicting Homer, Socrates, Plato, and Demosthenes on the bell tower standing in front of us. At a hundred feet tall, it's made from granite, its carvings of Portland stone.

To my left is Trinity Chapel and to my right is the Examination Hall. Simone drags me over to the Old Library building. During the day, visitors are sweating, scrambling to get inside. Now the place is deserted and the air is cool.

The moon is out and it feels strange walking around the grounds at this time of night. Up ahead I see Nocturnal's security man, built like a bull. He's wearing a baggy brown suit and standing outside the main entrance of the Old Library.

"Where is he?" I ask the security man. He gawks down at the Simone.

"Inside," he replies. The whole situation feels rather strange. Nocturnal must have contacts in high places to be able to waltz in without a ticket.

There's nobody around to stop me or to ask me what business I have being here. The souvenir shop is closed and the lights are off. The place is dark as I walk up to the library.

I'm taken aback by the sheer size of the picturesque library as we enter. The Jedi Temple Library in the movie *Star Wars: Episode II—Attack of the Clones* looks awfully similar.

"Welcome to the Long Room," a voice booms behind me. "Considered to be one of the most beautiful libraries in the world. The library chamber houses two hundred thousand books, mostly ancient."

Nocturnal emerges from the dark wearing a black suit and copper-colored cravat with hints of violet. By my feet I can hear Simone growl at him.

"What are ye now, a tour guide in the evenings?" I say. He walks closer to me, the dim light shining on his pale white face.

"Extraordinary, isn't it?" he says looking around the library, hands behind his back. He isn't wrong. I can't take me eyes off the barrel-vaulted ceiling, the many marble busts of writers and great philosophers, and the overwhelming stalls of books. "Built between 1712 and 1732 with a collection of books from the fifteenth to the eighteenth century. They raised the roof of the gallery in 1860 to shelve more books from the nineteenth century."

We begin to walk the length of the library. The whiff of the leather-bound books is a joy, but I could do without the squeaking floorboards. I look up at the balconies. Each bookcase is roped off.

Elaborate gold letters are painted on the sides of the stalls, and wooden ladders as tall as two-story houses reach the top shelf. The brown leather books look dense and large. It must have cost a fortune to print them.

"Is this why you invited me here, to give me a tour of the Old Library?"

"Of course not, but it's a lovely location to meet." I catch Simone staring intently at a bust of Sir Isaac Newton.

"How was your circus event the other night? I hope Ruby Collins wasn't mistreated."

"Unfortunately, the event was cut short due to the fire alarm going off. My guests were drenched in water from the sprinklers."

"What an awful shame."

"But I have a feeling you already knew that," he says.

"Isn't this a beautiful harp," I say, changing the subject. I lean forward, holding the leash in my hand, staring intently into a glass box containing a harp.

"Ireland's oldest harp," he says. The bust of Jonathan Swift is listening in on our conversation.

"So, why am I here?"

"Lorcan Doyle."

"What about him?"

"The news report says he was shot twice in the head with a .44 Magnum revolver. They found the gun a few hours ago," he says with his eyes on me. "Nobody witnessed his body being dragged from his garden office to the river Dodder in a suitcase. Curious, isn't it?"

"In what way?"

"It seemed like a professional hit," he says.

"Are you implying something? Even if I was involved with that hit, it's confidential." I comb my beard with my hand. "But just to let you know, I had nothing to do with his murder."

"Of course. The Bronze Man runs a tight ship. I heard the roof of her bar collapsed, such a pity. I planned on visiting next week."

"I'm sure she'll figure it out, she always does."

"Who do you think murdered Lorcan Doyle?"

"What I've heard is that he was a dirty little fella, but I think you already knew that. I'm sure he's visited your dungeon before."

"I detest the word *dungeon*. I use words like *escapism, tranquility... pleasure* to describe my workplace. And to answer your question, Lorcan was a customer of mine. He owed me some money."

"How much?"

"Thirty grand."

"That's a filthy amount," I say.

"See, I trusted him to pay up because he could have been easily blackmailed and I was on the verge of doing that until he got killed. Whoever shot him has really pissed me off."

"I heard he had dealings with the McCarthys. They might have done it."

"Maybe, but why kill an important contact? How about you go sniffing around and find out who ordered the hit, I'm very curious." I nod. "You probably know by now, but me and Olivia had a chat earlier today."

"You shouldn't have told her about our agreement."

"You ruined my circus event the other night. I was very upset. Besides, you can't be a killer and be in a relationship. That's nothing but a fantasy."

"This is my last job I do for you. Can we shake on that?" I ask him. He reaches out his frail hand. I shake his hand quickly and start leaving. "Come on, Simone, let's go."

"I want some juicy news, Patrick, you hear me!"

~~TRINITY COLLEGE LIBRARY~~

CHAPTER TWENTY-EIGHT

All this running around for free doesn't feel right. I should be getting paid for it. The walk back home is long. My legs have had enough. I put on a pot of tea and open up my laptop. I start doing my research on the Shelbourne racetrack, studying the map and all the entrance and exit points.

I screenshot photos of Dylan McCarthy on my phone. The Bison obviously wants to disrupt the McCarthys' operations. Killing Lorcan Doyle was step one. Lorcan's power to pass containers on the port is a big deal, and killing Dylan McCarthy feels like the final nail in the coffin.

I research any enemies the McCarthys might have. There's a small-time gang operating out of County Longford run by the Barnes Brothers. Not too long ago, one of the brothers got into a scuffle at a bar with one of the members of the McCarthys' gang. Another article says the McCarthys had a bad deal with a Moroccan gang last year—the McCarthys didn't pay in full for product.

There isn't a lot of time to be limping about with my dick in my hand, trying to find answers, because this time tomorrow Dylan McCarthy needs to be dead.

I take a look at me to-do list. Getting a gun is going to be difficult. Jack is my main man for anything weapon related, especially on short notice.

I go through the few contacts I have and see the last person in the world I want help from. I give the contact a text: *Hey, I need your help.* A reply comes flying in on my phone: *I'm at 5 Dunsink Lane.*

I put my slippers back on, pet Simone on the couch, and leave. I can get to the location in about twenty minutes if I cycle at a good pace. The route takes me through Stoneybatter, Cabra, Ashtown, and not far from Blanchardstown. To be honest, I'm not too familiar with the area—it's away from the big smoke.

In a matter of minutes, I'm cycling through tight country roads and I'm surrounded by fields. Giant tree branches droop over the roads like long, slender fingers, and crinkled leaves blow in the wind.

The roads are calm, but it can feel like I'm on a Formula One track in Istanbul with all these tight bends. The occasional car has to overtake me, which is asking for trouble. I hit my brakes, which make a distressing squeaking sound.

The road sign ahead of me reads: **DUNSINK**. I turn right. It takes me down on a long straight road. I'm not seeing any houses down in these woodlands and the lighting is poor.

The Dunsink Observatory is close by. I see the copper-roofed dome as I slow down. I can picture it opening up and a large telescope pointing to the sky. You would be lucky to get a clear day in Ireland.

I stare at my phone, holding it up high like it's a metal detector. The signal keeps going in and out. I stop on the side of the road and get off my bike, locking it around a sign that says **NO DUMPING PERMITTED, MAX FINE €3000**. What kind of person would dump their shit in the woods? Then I remember seeing mattresses, sofas, and cookers left out on the side of the road. And when Halloween comes around, you'll find them in a bonfire.

I continue to walk for about two minutes. Something lurks in the trees. I can hear it jumping on the branches, watching me. The ground has tire tracks turning into a small property down a muddy hill. I see lights on.

I don't want my slippers getting dirty so I try to avoid the tracks and walk in the grass. The property is a bungalow. Above the entrance there's a wind vane in the form of a rooster. There's a car in the driveway. It looks brand-new.

I tap the knocker twice on the door. Nothing. Then a shadow passes the window. I wait patiently in the dark.

"Put your hands up!" says a deep voice behind me, and I feel a gun pressing against the back of my neck. I turn around quickly.

"It's me, you gobshite," I say to him. Standing in front of me is Eagle Eye. It's been a few months since we last spoke. His beard has grown out, the color dark gray. The fringe on his head is sticking up like he just rolled out of bed. "What's wrong with you?"

"I have a situation." Eagle Eye lowers his gun.

"So do I," I say. "I need a gun."

"Help me first."

"How bad are we talking?" I ask. I noticed now that his knuckles are red and cut up.

"Real bad. Let me show you." Eagle Eye opens up the front door wide but doesn't enter, still holding on to the door handle. I poke my head inside, also not entering. It's warm. I do a quick glance around the bungalow. I count three dead bodies. One at a computer desk with a bullet in his head, the second one lying on the kitchen table with at least eight stabs to his chest, and the third one with his head smashed to pieces with the fridge door. There's a mixture of milk and blood on the floor tiles in the kitchen.

I stick my head back outside in the cold air. Eagle Eye gently closes the door as if he doesn't want to wake up the dead.

"It's a bleedin' massacre in there." I feel my jaw tense up. "What happened?"

He scratches the gun on the side of his head. "The fat bloke with the bullet in his head was released from prison last month for kiddy porn."

"And the other two?"

"The one on the kitchen table came out from the toilet. We got into a scrap and I ended up dropping my gun and grabbing the kitchen knife, stabbing him. I didn't see that coming because I scoped this place out for like two weeks and never saw anyone come in or out except for the pedo."

"And the third fella?"

"I took a deep breath, sat down for a few minutes, and bloke number three enters the bungalow. We got in a scuffle and I end up bashing his head in with the fridge door," he says casually.

"I'm assuming this was supposed to be an in-and-out job?"

"The boss said to be discreet and don't make a scene," he says.

"It's like a bleedin' Tarantino movie in there." I feel the cold wind hit my face. "What are we gonna do?"

"I was going to burn this dump to the ground, but that might invite unwanted attention," he says.

"It sure would. What if we dump all the bodies elsewhere?"

"Too risky. Ideally, I don't want three dead bodies in my car on the roads at this time of night. I'm not in a mood to be pulled over and caught up in a shootout with the Garda. I don't plan to be in the news this week. There's enough headlines in the papers to worry about."

"You mean the dead body on the Dodder?"

"Exactly," he says, waving his gun, then putting it away.

"You know who this killer is?"

"All I know is that this psycho has a vendetta on someone. Body in a fuckin' suitcase, I thought it was the work of the Lemon Man when I heard about it," he says. We both stand silently for a moment.

"We do a *Pulp Fiction*."

"A what?"

"*Pulp Fiction*, the movie? Do you remember the infamous Harvey Keitel scene?" He looks at me like I have two heads. "We wipe down everything inside the bungalow, spotless clean. Not a drop of blood to be seen."

"And the bodies?"

"We leave the pedo where he is and bury the other two out in the field," I say.

Eagle Eye touches his knuckles, thinking hard about the idea. He nods in approval.

We start with the two bodies, picking them up one at a time. I grab the ankles while Eagle Eye lifts under the armpits of victim number two. He's heavy. We get outside. Not too far from us are cows, sheep, and the rotten smell of manure.

We get two shovels from the garden shed and start digging. It takes us an hour to dig two holes deep enough for the bodies.

My arms and legs are covered in dirt. Eagle Eye is sweating and breathing heavily. We throw victim number two into the hole. We go back inside the bungalow and grab victim number three, with the smashed-up face—similar to something you see in a Picasso painting. His nose is broken, his cheekbones are cut up, and his skull is in bad shape. I can even see his brains seeping out like a rhubarb pie. We dump him in the second hole and pour the dirt in, filling it up. My arms are burning and my lower back is tightening up. This is the third body I've buried this week. They should really be calling me the feckin' gravedigger.

We drag our tired bodies back inside. I check the cabinets and get two bottles of bleach, three sponges, and countertop cleaner.

Eagle Eye gets a bucket and mop from the cupboard and starts cleaning the floors. I wipe the kitchen down from top to bottom. I do it another three times. Eagle Eye is on his knees scrubbing the fridge door with a smiley-face sponge. When he squeezes it over the bucket of water, the water changes color to a murky red.

The place is now blood-free. Eagle Eye is finished and dumps the bloody water down the bathtub. He puts the knife in the bucket. I tie up a black plastic bag filled with dirty kitchen towels and cleaning supplies. We leave all the windows open in the bungalow and turn off the lights.

"I'll take that off ye," he says, gesturing to the plastic bag in my hand. I give it to him. We go outside and put everything in his black Audi. It has a sporty build to it. "Need a lift?"

"Sure." I throw my bike in his trunk. The interior of his car is immaculate with the scent of pine. The car ride is smooth when we get on the road. Eagle Eye doesn't look like he's in the mood for small talk.

We enter Smithfield Square, and Eagle Eye parks the car outside the main entrance. He reaches into his jacket pocket, pulls out a SIG Sauer pistol, and hands it to me.

"We good?" I ask. He responds with a soft nod. I get out of the car. "I'll see you around." I remove my bike from the trunk and shut the door. Then Eagle Eye drives off.

Ten o'clock. I'm a broken man. I look up at the endless skies and see the pretty stars glistening. All I want is a shower and to slide into to a warm bed.

~~GUN II~~

CHAPTER TWENTY-NINE

The next morning. I had one of the worst sleeps of my life. I tossed and turned all night long. Even the dog had enough of me and dragged herself downstairs.

I had horrific dreams of Jack being tortured by three men. What was strange was that they were all wearing animal masks. One of them had a rabbit mask on his face like something out of *The Wicker Man*. He was poking Jack in the ribs with a sharp blade.

All I could hear were loud screams coming from Jack's mouth as his bloodied body was tied to a chair with barbed wire. Eventually the screaming stopped and Jack's chin fell. The men in masks laughed hysterically, dancing around his dead body.

Waking up in an empty bed is a horrible feeling. I miss Olivia terribly. I pull my body out of bed with great discomfort and have a cold shower. It wakes me up a little.

I put on fresh clothing and use the hair dryer for my long hair. My beard is bushier than normal and could do with a trim. I tie my hair in a low man bun. The morning is still young, so I can't eat until twelve if I'm going to keep this fasting up.

I fill the dog's bowl up with fresh water and another with food. I drop an electrolyte tablet into a pint glass with water. I watch it dissolve and turn green. I lash it back along with my painkiller. I've only three pills left in the bottle.

I make sure the fanny pack is packed and ready to go. The SIG Sauer pistol is fully loaded and fits nicely inside.

I leave the building with my bike. The older lady is at the front desk this morning drinking her usual black coffee, which makes me want to puke. I call Junkie Jake.

"What's up?" he says.

"Are ye around?" I ask JJ.

"I'm actually in town."

"Drop over to us in Smithfield."

"I'll be there in few minutes… Fuckin' traffic!" he yells over the cry of an ambulance, and he hangs up.

Junkie Jake pulls up in Smithfield Square in a blue Ford Fiesta that has seen better days. The passenger's door opens up.

"Get in!" he shouts.

"Why?"

"Just get in, I need a hand with something." He is red-faced and wearing an Adidas track suit. I leave my bike locked across from the Cobblestone pub.

"What's wrong?" I ask him as I sit down in the passenger's seat. The car is roasting inside and smells of wild cherry and McDonald's.

"Me bleedin' sister again. She's always complaining about the ex-boyfriend. He was supposed to pick up his son this morning for school. This guy is a real prick!" JJ's upper gum flares as he grips the steering wheel tightly. "I swear to God, wait until I get me hands on that little cunt."

"I have your money."

"He's a little lowlife," JJ replies under his breath.

We turn hard on Parnell Street. I feel my shoulder push against the window and my bruised hip dig into the seat belt. We pull up outside a pet shop.

"There's the rat now," JJ says and jumps out of the car, slamming the door behind him.

He runs across the tram tracks. I watch the action unfold. He approaches a couple holding hands. He grabs the young man wearing a denim jacket by the collar, throwing him on the ground. JJ pulls him across the tracks and throws him in the back seat of the Ford Fiesta.

"Jesus Christ, JJ, what the fuck ye doin'?" the bloke says. He must be in his early twenties, his fringe wet and flattened with gel.

"What I'm doing?" JJ says. "You should be dropping off your son to school right now."

"Ah, I'm after forgettin' all about it," he replies.

"That's not good enough, pal," JJ says. "I'm sick of ye. My sister is crying to me all morning about you being a shitty father and a waste of fuckin' space."

"It's not my fault, I swear. It's tough out there. The economy has gone to shit."

"But you have time to spend with that slag, don't ye?" JJ shouts.

"Leave Joanne out of this, will ye?"

"Shut your mouth. You better get your shit together this week or I'm going to break your fuckin' legs. You won't able to go on long walks with that tramp you're seeing!"

"Ha, you wouldn't be able hurt a fly." The bloke snickers.

"I won't, but this fella beside me will." JJ points at me.

"He looks about sixty," the young fella replies. I'm sick to death of people calling me old, so I unzip me fanny pack and remove the SIG Sauer pistol and point it at him. "What the fuck are you doing!"

"Lock the doors," I say to JJ. The young fella tries to pull on the door handle but it's too late. I stroke the hair on me chin.

"I'm not going to lie to ye, I am due a good trimming." I shake the gun at him. "What JJ said was wrong. I won't break your legs. I'll take ye far away into the Wicklow Mountains... you should see them, they're spectacular. Then I'll shoot both your kneecaps right off." I press the gun into the young fella's knee. "After that, I'll leave you there in the wilderness all by yourself."

The disbelief on his face is priceless. He might piss himself. Even JJ is stunned.

I press the gun harder into his knee. "Now, you make sure your son is taken care of, ye hear me?" I say. "Because I'm not a fan of deadbeat fathers, I despise them. I would gladly shoot you for free."

The young fella is now trembling with fear. "I will," he says. "I'll get my shit together this week, I promise."

"That's a good lad, because we don't want to see you in a wheelchair, do we?" I say. The young man shakes his head. "Now, get the fuck out of here."

JJ unlocks the door and the bloke goes running off.

"What was that all about?" JJ asks as we watch the rat scurry across the road, pulling up his jeans. "Kneecapping in Wicklow Mountains, Jaysus."

"It worked, didn't it? I have your money here." I hand him the cash.

JJ folds the bills into his pocket. "Did you pay Neil Flanagan a visit?"

"Yeah. He said he had nothing to do with the killing of Lorcan Doyle."

"Sounds about right, they don't have the bottle to pull off a hit like that."

"What do you know about the McCarthys?" I say. "I heard they had a run-in with the Barnes Brothers from County Longford."

"It wouldn't be smart for the Barnes Brothers to be challenging the McCarthys, they're not as well-connected or strong enough to be going to war."

"And this Moroccan gang? I heard the McCarthys didn't pay them in full for some product."

"It's only come out that most of the Moroccan gang are going to be doing some hard time."

"What do you mean?"

"Turns out there was a rat in the gang," JJ says.

"Jesus."

"I'll tell you one thing, the killing of Lorcan Doyle has disrupted a lot of business for the McCarthys. This attack sounds very personal."

"I read the son Dylan is coming over from Spain for a visit."

"Yeah, I saw that," JJ says. "The father is probably begging him to be involved in the business. He's a smart lad. Went to university and everything... and speaks five languages."

"Do you know anybody who would have an idea who'd want to take down the McCarthys?"

"Let me think... Do you remember Cracksman Charlie?"

"The robber?" I say.

"Yeah. He just got out of prison six months ago. He did a year for cannabis possession... worked with the McCarthys back in the nineties, and not only that... Lorcan Doyle was the one who arrested him," JJ says, then looks at himself in the rearview mirror. "Jesus Christ."

"What is it?"

"I used this new face wash this morning, now me face is all red like a feckin' strawberry."

~~JUNKIE JAKE~~

CHAPTER THIRTY

ast month I was watching a documentary film on the TV called *The Greatest Robberies of Ireland*. One of the episodes was called "Cracksman Charlie."

The film crew interviewed him and everything, right in his house. He talked about his days accused of being a robber. The interviewer and Charlie walked around the area he lives in. I remember the sign behind him in the documentary. It read **WELCOME TO MARINO**.

My day isn't over yet. JJ drops me off at Smithfield and I begin traveling north. The conditions are still dry but the winds are picking up. They assault me like the waves at the Forty Foot in Sandycove. Weaving in and out of cars, I make it to Amiens Street, which takes me all the way to Marino.

I secure my bike in front of a dermatologist. Next door is a beauty salon and a barber. I walk inside the barber. The doorbell above my head rings. I get a whiff of shaving cream, hair tonic, and cheap aftershaves.

There's an old fella about eighty years old getting his white hair trimmed by a slim young fella with sleeve tattoos and a messy quiff. The young man looks me up and down.

A small TV showing golf is on in the corner of the room. Rory McIlroy is in the crouching position, eyeing up a twenty-yard putt for a birdie.

"What can I do ye for?" asks a middle-aged bloke reading the newspaper on a brown leather couch. He's wearing a light-blue denim apron, and his hairstyle is a classic side part.

"I need me beard trimmed," I say to him.

"Sure thing." He folds his newspaper and gets off the couch. "Take a seat." The barber throws the gown up in the air before it gently lands on my body like a parachute. He tightens it around my neck, pressing against my Adam's apple. He begins combing my beard. The hair pulls on my skin. It's knotted from all the twisting I do to it throughout the day. "Are you sure you don't want the hair on your head trimmed?"

"I'm sure."

There's a sterilizing glass jar on the countertop with blue liquid inside. A comb and a pair of scissors are floating in it. I look to my left and see the old man getting his hair trimmed. His right hand is trembling on his knee. He's wearing a yellow-gold claddagh ring.

"Your call," he says, holding a six-and-a-half-inch stainless steel scissors in his hand. "I'm gonna tidy up the cheek area on your face and clean up the upper lip."

"The mustache can be a nuisance when I'm eating."

"You're not from around here, are ye?"

"No, I live in the city."

"Ah, it's too bloody expensive in there," says the old man beside me, shaking his head. "I've seen a studio apartment going for three grand a month... tiny thing it was. And ye had to share a bathroom in the building. Shocking... a terrible tragedy for anyone trying to live there."

"Will ye keep still," says the tattooed barber to the old man.

"Those bloody politicians are a disgrace," the old man says. "They're all dumb as nails. It's their fault my children can't buy a bloody house near me. They have to live miles away. Meath, Offaly, or Carlow. Nothing feckin' out in the country," he says. "Sure, who wants to be livin' out there?"

"Have you ever thought they left Dublin to get away from you?" the barber says, cutting my barbaric mustache.

"Feck off!" he responds. "You think you're funny, don't ye?"

"I'm just telling the truth. They didn't want to hear your moaning all the time."

The old man pouts his wrinkled lips together. A few quiet seconds go by. Loud cheers are coming from the TV, then he says, "How can ye watch that awful sport? Would put ye right to sleep."

"What brings you to Marino?" the barber asks me, turning on the hair clipper, which makes a vicious electric sound in my ear like I'm in *The Texas Chainsaw Massacre*.

"I'm looking for someone... Cracksman Charlie," I say. The barber turns the clipper off. I watch the two barbers glance at each other in the mirror. Their faces stone-cold.

"We don't know who he is," he says.

"Sure ye do. He lives in the area, doesn't he?"

"What do you want with him?"

"I'm a distant friend of his. I need to talk to him," I say.

The barber takes two steps back. "I reckon you should leave."

"Sure you need to finish me beard off. You've only done half of it." I touch the one side he trimmed.

"Not today. You need to leave and I'm not going to ask ye again."

"Ah, don't be so sour. I'm an old friend of Charlie's." I stand up with the gown still on me. Hair trickles down to the floor.

"Get out," he shouts at me.

I rip the gown off me neck, letting it drop to the floor, full of hair. I reach into me fanny pack and remove a crisp ten-euro note. I tear it in half and throw one piece on the chair and put the other half back in my fanny pack.

"For a half job."

I leave the barber's a little peeved-off. It probably wouldn't be a good idea to be going door-to-door asking for this Charlie bloke. Word gets around fast. I go over to my bike, deflated. I hear the bell ring behind me from the barber. I turn to see the old man standing outside the barber with his walking stick and tweed cap.

"He lives by the park... the big circular one." The old man points with his stick. "Go straight. Keep an eye out for the yellow door."

The old man turns the corner and vanishes.

I follow the instructions the old fella gives me. I leave my bike locked up and walk on Fairview Lower. It brings me to Marino Park. At the center of the field is a football pitch with trees that have long, thick branches you could do pull-ups on.

The housing estate looks like something from the 1920s and 1930s. The houses all face the circular park. I need to do a lap. I pass by a house with a mint-green front door, and the neighbor on the corner has a flamingo-pink one.

Jesus Christ, there are some hideous-colored doors out here. But that isn't the only odd thing. There's a house with garden gnomes and angel statues, dozens of them, all scattered around the lawn. I also hear the annoying sounds of wind chimes.

I'm literally walking around in circles. My left leg is starting to cramp up.

Then I see it. My neck straightens up like an alpaca. The yellow door. Sticking out like the sun emerging from the clouds. It brightens up the street. I walk over and push the rusty gate open. It makes a horrific whining noise. I walk up to the flashy-colored front door. Just as I'm about to give it a good walloping, it opens up wide.

A young teenager is standing in front of me. She has dyed blond hair and a piercing under her lower lip and is caked in fake tan. A white Siberian cat runs out from the house, stepping over my feet.

"Who are you?" she asks in a deep inner-city tone.

"I'm looking for Charlie."

"He's not talking to anyone," she says. "He's already spoken to the Garda."

"I'm not the Garda."

"Then you must be a scummy journalist. You bastards have some nerve showing up here at our front door," she says, getting riled up, her hands on her lower back like she's pregnant.

I am losing patience. "I'm not a bleedin' journalist. Can ye just get me Charlie."

She looks me up and down. "How much is in it for me?"

"Ye want money?"

"Yeah. Me and my friend want to see Dua Lipa at the end of the year," she says.

"Jaysus. How's fifty sound?"

"You're having a laugh, aren't yeah? Sure, that would only get yeah one ticket and the bus in."

I reach back into my fanny pack and hand her another fifty. "Will that do?"

"It will do." She snatches the money from my hand. She steps out from the door and pats me down. "He's out back. Go through the side entrance around the back. Make sure to push hard on the door, it can be a bit stiff."

The young girl slams the front door so hard that the gold bird knocker makes a loud *thump*.

I'm a lucky man. She didn't snoop in me fanny pack.

I walk around to the side of the house. I come to a beaten-up wooden door with the paint falling off. I use my shoulder to push through as I turn the handle. The door scrapes off the ground. I maneuver my way through the bed linen hanging on the washing lines. The wind sweeps them up in the air. The scent is glorious.

The back garden is very long. In the distance I see sheds of sorts and hear the sounds of birds chirping. As I slowly approach, I see there's a massive bird aviary in the shape of a dome at the back. It covers the width of the garden. I peek through the fence, squinting. There're multiple thin branches sprawling out from a tree, with colorful birds perched on them.

"That one up there is an eastern bluebird," says a raspy voice beside me.

I turn. Standing beside me is a red-faced man with messy curly brown hair and a hairline that stretches all the way back, like Colm Meaney when he was in *Star Trek: The Next Generation*.

"Did ye know there's these gypsy moths, which lay eggs on trees across North America. They release a toxin and it destroys the trees. But there's a solution... birds," he says, smiling at me with kind eyes. He's holding a glass jar you would fill with honey. This one has moths fluttering around inside. He opens the gate attached to the aviary and goes inside. "Male moths can track down a female three hundred feet away with their antennas."

"I never knew that," I say.

"There's even this moth called the hummingbird hawk-moth, which uses its long tongue to suck out the nectar from flowers. Eleven inches long. Mad, isn't it?"

"I'm not here for a natural history lesson, I can watch that at home on the telly."

"You're no journo?"

"I'm not."

"Then who are you?"

"I've heard you were released from prison six months ago," I say.

"I was set up," he says. "I keep telling the papers, but they won't listen."

"How were you set up?"

"That commissioner prick always hated my guts."

"Lorcan Doyle?"

"Yeah."

"Why?"

He looks me up and down.

"You saw me daughter earlier. She patted you down good, didn't she?" he asks. I nod. "Then you're not a rat." He plucks one of the moths from the jar. He holds the moth's wing and feeds it to a bird. "Back in the day I *allegedly* did some house robberies around Dublin, mainly wealthy areas. They said I broke into a posh home out in Killiney and tied up a couple and robbed them. They said I wasn't there for the jewelry or money laying around, I was there for the paintings."

"Which ones?"

"Apparently, I wasn't interested in the nineteen-century bullshit art they had but that I was eyeing up Andy Warhol's *Ingrid Bergman with Hat* and Roy Lichtenstein's *Red Lamp*," he says. "Lorcan wanted me to go down so badly, see, he was close friends with the couple who got robbed. Twenty years later I get pulled over by Lorcan for possession of cannabis. He sends me away for six months. The cunt set me up, planted the drugs in me car."

"Is that why you killed Lorcan?"

"I didn't do such a thing. Sure, I wouldn't have the bleedin' time to be stuffin' dead bodies in suitcases," he says, all flustered, even redder. "I'll tell ye this. I've never hurt a soul in my entire life and there's no way I would risk doing something mad like that."

"What about getting someone else to do it for you?" It goes quiet between us. The birds are still twittering away and it stinks of shit everywhere.

"I wouldn't have the stomach to do it. Way too risky."

"Did someone ever come to you asking about the commissioner?"

"Now that I think about it, a woman in her thirties dropped by... this must have been a month ago, I think. She was asking about Lorcan and his whereabouts. Strange-looking lady."

"Why did she come to you?"

"She knew I had dealings with Lorcan, but I wasn't the only one who had it out for him. Lorcan's hands were always covered in dirt." He removes another moth from the jar. The wing starts vibrating between his fingertips.

"And the woman? You said she was strange?"

"She had a look to her that didn't sit right. Like she'd been someplace dark. She had a scar down the middle of her eyelid. Sure, I get the occasional visit from family members I've *allegedly* robbed over the years, so it was no surprise."

"Did ye get a name?"

"Nope. I told her to fuck right off," he says. "And I think you've talked to me enough today."

"Last question. How much were those paintings worth?"

"They would have been worth a lot more money today. But at the time, they were enough to pay off a house in an inner suburb on the Northside of Dublin." He winks.

As I leave the garden, I see a man in his late forties, shaved head, standing at the back porch wearing a pair of red-and-white Air Jordans and holding a bottle of Peroni beer. Then I see the Siberian cat sitting on the wall, licking its paws.

CHAPTER THIRTY-ONE

I have no more time to be snooping around asking questions that could get me into trouble. Whoever has it out for Lorcan Doyle and the McCarthys has it out for me too. They know who I am and my relationship with Jack.

My brain feels like it's turned to soup. There're way too many victims and family members I've probably pissed off over the years, and for the McCarthys it's even worse. I'm not fuckin' Dexter who keeps blood samples of his every victim in an air conditioner. I don't record every hit or every threat I've done in the past.

I get on my bike and head back into town, pedaling to my next location. The pain in my hip is still gnawing at me. The sun is dying down and temperatures are dropping. I stop at a traffic light and see two women holding hands. I think of Olivia and the shit I've put her through. Maybe I don't deserve her.

I cycle past the Custom House on the quays. The neoclassical eighteenth-century building is picturesque and visitors across the Liffey eye up the perfect photo. I drift over Talbot Memorial Bridge, which commemorates members of the Dublin Brigade who died during the Irish War of Independence.

The cycling lane goes up on the path beside Talbot Memorial Bridge, which is kind of dangerous. I almost clip a bloke pushing a stroller. I hear him giving out to his child: "That's it, no more sweets! You're going to have no teeth left."

My forearms burn and the bones in my hands ache as I grip the handlebars. I turn left onto City Quay. It's quiet around this area of Dublin, even though it has one of the best views of the Liffey and the Samuel Beckett Bridge.

There's also a diving bell, thirteen meters tall, ninety tons, resembling the sword of Excalibur stuck in a rock. Since most people work from home, the glass office buildings are empty during the week.

There're young children sailing in the water on my left as I take a right on Forbes Street. The road is smoother than most parts of Dublin.

I lock my bike outside a deli on Sir John Rogerson's Quay and run inside before it closes up. I buy a turkey club sandwich and a Portuguese custard tart. I feel like I haven't eaten enough greens this week, so I grab a green vegetable juice. It has kale, spinach, celery, cucumber, and ginger. It all sounds too healthy, but I need it in my system. I eat it all.

The Shelbourne racetrack opens up in thirty minutes. Stuffed after the sandwich, I get back on my bike and begin pedaling toward the racetrack. I pass my old apartment building on the Grand Canal Dock. I take a left, cycling hard over Mac Mahon Bridge, and end up on Ringsend Road. I make it to the Shelbourne racetrack. I can hear rowdy herds of people lining up outside to get inside. I leave my bike around a speed limit sign pole.

I make my way inside the racetrack. The atmosphere resembles a scene from Stanley Kubrick's *The Killing*. There's security walking about at the entrance in hi-vis waterproof security jackets. I sneak in behind a pack of lively lads and head straight for the restrooms.

I step inside one of the stalls, lock the door behind me, and unzip my fanny pack. I make sure the gun is loaded. I place it back inside and leave. I notice the sink tap to my right is turned on. Water wasting away. I immediately turn it off.

A young fella comes out of the stall, goggled-eyed. He turns the tap on and water splashes all over his plain white shirt. He reeks of beer and cigarettes.

"Don't be betting on Lightning Legend. I don't trust him."
He looks in the mirror. "If I was you, I would put your money on
Uncle Buck." He pats his wet hands against his black slacks. "He's
a winner for sure."

"Thanks for the tip."

I leave the restrooms in a hurry, flustered. I need to get my
shit together.

There's over a thousand people moving about, gambling and
drinking. I hear the long roar of a Boeing 747 in the sky above
me. It leaves behind a vapor trail as the sun goes down. The lights
flicker on the wings between the dark clouds. The Aviva Stadium
is across the racetrack, shaped like a bedpan.

A race is about to begin. Spectators gather near the fence on
the racetrack. I feel my forehead starting to sweat. I roll up my
sleeves, folding them at the elbow. The greyhounds start sprinting. The commentator is bellowing out from the speakers.

I look up at the big screen. The slender dogs move with such
grace around the bend, they almost touch each other as they
chase the mechanical stuffed rabbit.

"Number 6 and 2 are immediately off to a good start," the commentator says rapidly. "Queen Bee having problems on the inside."

The muzzle doesn't cover their razor-sharp teeth, as they
growl from their wet mouths. Paws bounce off the sand, creating small dust clouds. Not an ounce of fat on their bodies. Their
muscles are protruding from their skin like a bodybuilder posing
on the Mr. Olympia stage.

The mobs of spectators start shouting, cheering the dogs on,
waving their betting slips in the air. Their faces become deranged
and purple in color. They're spilling beer out of plastic cups as the
greyhounds approach the final bend.

"Number 4 Bingo Blitzer and Lightning Legend… neck and
neck," shouts the commentator.

"Go on, ye good thing!" roars an old man wearing a tweed
flat cap.

"Uncle Buck is catching up to the pack on the outside...Lightning Legend has fallen! And Uncle Buck is going to take the win at a massive ten to one!" the commentator screams, almost losing his voice. Ripped-up betting slips are thrown up in the air like confetti.

If Dylan McCarthy is going to be anywhere, it's the private suites. I skip through the crowds and start walking up some stairs. I reach the top out of breath.

"Sorry," says somebody bumping into me. I see the man's face. Jesus Christ, it's Dylan McCarthy. I follow him. He enters one of the private suites, which must have ten or so lads inside. There's also two security men by the door.

A slender middle-aged woman stops me.

"This is a private party," she says.

"Sorry, I'm on the wrong floor," I reply, acting the eejit. I look at the race times on the monitors. They are on every twenty minutes. Tonight, they have a total of six races. I sit down, keeping my eye on the boisterous party in the private suite. I need to get Dylan by himself somehow.

There's a parking lot on the far side of the racetrack. I head in that direction. I put my face mask on, getting a final glimpse of the mountains in the distance as the massive floodlights turn on.

It's quiet when I arrive in the parking lot. I see five coaches parked beside one another, all empty. The stones crunch under my slippers as I make my way over to the parked vehicles. I see a bloke about fifty or so sitting in a black Cadillac Escalade with all the windows down, playing Franz Schubert.

The driver sticks his head out the window. "Are you lost?"

"No, I was supposed to meet me mate Dylan here," I reply through my face mask.

"Dylan McCarthy?" He steps out of the shiny Cadillac. His suit is gray and the trousers are wrinkled. The little hair he has on his head is slicked back with lots of waxy gel.

"Yeah, he said to meet me down here in the car park... I've tried ringing him but no answer."

"I'm his driver for tonight, I can try giving him a ring."

"Is that right." I quickly unzip my fanny pack and remove the gun and point it at the driver. "Now, I want you to call up Dylan and tell him to come down to the car park by himself. Tell him it's an emergency."

The driver gets his phone out from his pocket and calls Dylan. The classical music by Franz Schubert is still playing in the background, which is fitting because it's like we're in a waiting room. There's silence between us.

"It wouldn't be smart to be messing around with the McCarthys."

"You should keep your mouth shut," I say. "I don't want to have to put a bullet in your head."

In a few minutes, I see the shadowy figure of Dylan McCarthy coming my way. I now aim the gun at him.

"What's this all about?" he asks.

"Listen, I need to ask you a few questions."

"How dare you point that gun at me. Do you know who I am?"

"Who has it out for you?"

"You have some balls coming out here like this." Dylan is calm and collected like he's been in this situation before or he has something up his sleeve.

Then I hear the sound of stones crunching behind me. I quickly do a one-eighty and see a large fist plummeting toward my face for an instant before it connects with my cheekbone and the side of my nose. My legs give and I fall on the stones. The gun slips out of my hand, skittering under the Cadillac.

Dylan comes running over and kicks me ferociously in the stomach. "Motherfucker!" he barks. I feel the air leave my body. The guy who punched me must be six foot six. He picks me up with ease, tossing me against the vehicle. "Who the fuck are you?" Dylan shouts with fury in his eyes. The big fella punches me in the mouth.

"Answer him," the big fella yells out. "Hold him up," he says to the driver, who grabs me by the arms as the big fella throws another devastating punch, this time in the ribs. I can't breathe. Dylan rips the face mask off my mouth.

"Who sent you, old man?" Dylan asks.

I need to get out of this mess. I push my body back into the driver and leap my legs up, launching my feet into the big fella's face, knocking him onto the sharp stones. I swing my head back in a frenzy, walloping the driver's nose. He immediately lets go of me, falling on one knee, his face all bloodied. I throw a knee into his head and then a stabbing kick to the big fella's face.

Dylan locks eyes on me and makes a run for it. I jump onto the ground and search under the Cadillac for the gun. I get it and turn around just as the big fella is about to get up again. I put two bullets in his chest, then I turn to the driver.

"Please don't!" the driver pleads.

I don't hesitate and shoot him in the forehead.

I see Dylan running along the Dodder. I start chasing him down.

My body feels hot and heavy, like it's about to fold. My hoodie is glued to my skin and my legs are starting to buckle.

I see Dylan run under Ringsend Bridge. My breathing gets heavier, which hurts my stomach and ribs. To my left are walls of graffiti. Most of it random. Then I see a gigantic eye, lidless, with fire ejecting from it like a volcano erupting. Have I reached Mordor? Am I having a hallucinogenic experience? I see lots of bright colors surrounding me.

Beyond the walls is an abandoned ship, rotting and full of rust. **SAVE OUR SHIP** is spray-painted on the side. The lighting is horrendous. I can't see shit. I can hear Dylan but I can't see him now. I look around and his footsteps have stopped. I take a moment. Dylan is gone, but how? I walk along the bank. I come to a dead end. To my right is a scrapyard with old shipping containers.

With the gun in my hand, I go with caution. I press my hand on the sliding gate and enter the scrapyard. I can't hear a thing, not a whisper. I poke my head into one of the containers. It's black inside. The fucker could be anywhere.

I keep moving. Suddenly, a massive rat runs over my feet. I nearly pull the trigger.

Then I look up and see the figure of Dylan standing on top of the container. He jumps off, landing on me, and the gun goes flying out of my hand. Dylan is on top of me, digging his forearm into my face, putting all his weight on me. I feel like my cheekbone is going to cave in. He throws a venomous punch, hitting me perfectly over the eye. His breath, reeking of lager, is on my face, saliva dripping from his mouth.

He's stronger than me and my body is giving out. I can't hold him off any longer. Dylan latches his hands around my neck as I try reaching out for the gun. The stones are cutting my fingers as I grab a handful of them and smash them into his face. He falls off me. This is my chance. I jump on the gun, turn around, and shoot him twice in the chest. I slowly get up on my knees, breathing heavily, choking.

I get on my feet, and when I turn around Dylan is gone.

Fuck!

I panic and start searching. The floodlights come on in the scrapyard, blinding me. All I see is a puddle of blood on the stones. I follow the trail, leading to the locks on the river. I see a limping Dylan crossing over.

"Stop, Dylan!" I yell. He turns around holding his collarbone. Blood seeps through his fingertips. He has a bullet-proof vest on. I don't have time. I hear voices coming from the banks.

"Why?" he shouts back at me.

"Because I have no choice." I quickly shoot Dylan in the forehead. His neck whips back and his body falls over into the river Dodder. I hear his body splashing.

Running over, I remove my phone, quickly take a snap of Dylan floating in the Dodder, and send it to Jack's number. I fling the gun as far as possible into the river and escape the scene.

~~THE SHELBOURNE RACETRACK~~

CHAPTER THIRTY-TWO

Breathless, I lob myself onto my bike like a wounded cowboy slumped on a moving horse. I start pedaling. My face is throbbing with pain. I can hardly see out of my left eye. I cycle back into town feeling hefty raindrops fall on my face.

I get back to Smithfield a broken man and go straight up to the loft, ignoring the front desk lady. I pour myself a glass of cold water and swallow it back.

Simone is moaning at me, scraping her paw against my shin. I see a puddle of urine on the floor near the fridge. I quickly mop it up and open the balcony door so Simone can do a number two. I limp upstairs and look at myself in the bathroom mirror. My eye is swollen to the shape of a golf ball, and bruised like an orange. My stomach and ribs are tender to the touch. Dylan's savage kick stung me really good. Just when the bruise on my hip was healing up, another one appears. Half of my beard is trimmed, making me look like a right fool.

I strip down naked and take a warm shower. I dry myself and take another pill for the damage I've taken tonight. I lie down on the bed in my underwear with a bag of frozen veg on my eye and try to relax. The dog next to me is sulking as usual. I pet her down for a few minutes.

It's been a busy week of killing. First was Connor "The Savage" Dunphy at Mount Jerome Cemetery, then former commissioner Lorcan Doyle, and now Dylan McCarthy plus two of his goons. The worst part is that I only got paid for one kill. No, that isn't the worst of it. Olivia leaving me and Jack being tortured by these lunatics.

I close my eyes and try taking in slow, deep breaths. Darkness surrounds me. Then the floodlights come on, shining brightly on my face, making my vison blurry. I look down at my feet and see sand. It's cold on my skin. I'm just wearing my underwear. I hear something behind me, I turn my head and see a large box with colorful numbers ranging from one to eight. What's going on here? The lid shoots up and eight greyhounds begin sprinting out, chasing after me.

I start running for my life as the vicious greyhounds snap at my heels. They have no muzzles covering their razor-sharp teeth. Edging closer with their black beady eyes, salivating, viciously growling. My heart is pounding in my chest. My feet are sinking like I'm in quicksand.

The crowds are roaring with psychotic expressions on their faces, spitting and sticking out their tongues, laughing hysterically like demented clowns.

The finish line is strides away. My body tumbles over, pounding into the sand. I slowly lift my head up and see the greyhounds surrounding me, snarling. All at once they jump on me, latching their teeth into my skin.

I wake up. Simone is barking uncontrollably.

"What's wrong?" I ask her as the bag of frozen veg falls off my face. "Calm down, calm down," I say petting her body. Her body is shaking. I hear my phone vibrating on the bedside table. I pick it up. "Hello."

"Meet me at the Crazy Owl now!" the Bronze Man yells.

"What's wrong?"

"Just get over here." The call ends. Fuck. I quickly get dressed and wheel my bike out of the loft. I look at the time. One in the morning.

"See ye soon," I say to Simone as I close the door.

❧ ❧ ❧

Thursday morning. The town is alive and kicking. The streets are filled with people spilling out of the pubs. I arrive at the Crazy Owl and leave my bike locked outside. Slim is standing at the front entrance.

"Slim," I say to him.

"She's in the back," he replies. The bar still feels damp and cold. The hole in the ceiling is still not repaired.

I walk into the speakeasy and see Caitríona behind the bar, arms folded. I give her a nod. The Bronze Man is sitting in one of the booths. When I get closer, I see her face. She has a big shiner and swollen cheekbone.

"Jesus Christ, what happened to you?" I ask.

"I was going to ask you the same question."

I sit across from her. "Fell off me bike. Who did this to ye?"

"Thomas McCarthy."

"Why?"

"His son was murdered a few hours ago down at Shelbourne racetrack." She knocks back the last drop of whiskey left in her glass. She picks up the cigar and lighter but her hand is shaking. She slams them down on the table.

"Jaysus. What's that got to do with you?"

"He thinks I have something to do with the killing."

"Why would he think that?"

"The hit was professionally done. The driver and security man were also shot dead on site. Dylan was later discovered floating in the Dodder with the ducks."

"Or rats," Caitríona adds.

The Bronze Man scoops the ice cube from her glass, placing it on her eyelid. "Do you remember the hit you did eight years ago to William Hughes?"

"Vaguely," I reply.

"Thomas McCarthy was the one who ordered the hit. I said I never wanted to do business with them ever again," she says. "You do them a favor and they repay you by doing this." She drops the ice cube back in her glass and touches her wet face. "I'm scared, Patrick."

I never heard the Bronze Man say those words, ever, in the decade or so I've worked for her. I put my head in my hands, taking a deep breath.

"What's wrong?" she asks.

I pinch my bottom lip. "I need to tell you something."

"What is it?"

"Can I have a whiskey, Caitríona?" She comes around from the bar and drops a bottle of Midleton Very Rare on the table and pours the brown liquid into the two glasses. "Cheers," I say, colliding glasses with the Bronze Man. Then the words slip out. "I murdered Dylan McCarthy."

"What! What do you mean you murdered Dylan McCarthy?... Why?"

Caitríona slams her fist against the table, hurting her little finger in the process. "You bloody imbecile! We are all dead now."

"Calm down, you," the Bronze Man says to her. "I'm sure Patrick has a perfect explanation to why he might have us all killed."

"Jack has been taken."

"By who?"

"I've been trying to figure that out all week. This fella who goes by the name the Bison has taken Jack and had me kill Lorcan Doyle."

"The commissioner?" Caitríona says. "Christ Almighty."

"I didn't have a choice... if I didn't do it he was going to kill Jack." I show the Bronze Man photos of Jack tied up and bloodied on my phone.

"Oh my God." Caitríona pours another two glasses. As I'm about to grab mine, she picks it up and lashes it back.

"Why didn't you tell me sooner?" the Bronze Man asks.

"I panicked… I needed to act fast. I've been running around the city like a feckin' eejit trying to figure out who's done this. And I've been everywhere. Me head is all over the joint." I stand up with my hands in the pockets of my shorts.

"When will they let Jack go?"

"I don't bleedin' know. I've gotten no response yet."

"Everything has gone to shit," she says. "I've got the McCarthys on my back and now I have to shut the bar down."

"Shut the bar down?" I say.

"I've spent all me money on this place. There's nothing left." The Bronze Man looks defeated. Caitríona sits down on a stool. The three of us drained.

"How about this," I say. "We meet up with the McCarthys and cut a deal with them. Find this Bison fella and kill him. This will clear your name with them."

"Are you out of your mind!" Caitríona blurts out.

The Bronze Man looks up at me. "Let's do it."

"Are you serious?" Caitríona says.

"Big Tomo is going to be on our backs until he finds out who did it, and my bar needs saving. We need the money and proof we had nothing to do with the killings by bringing down this Bison fella."

"Arrange a meeting," I say to her and hand her a pill from my fanny pack. "Here, take one of these. It will help with the swelling."

"You got one for me?" asks Caitríona.

I leave the Crazy Owl.

CHAPTER THIRTY-THREE

I sit on the couch like a cracked vase. Simone's big head lies on my lap. I plan to stroke her ears until my eyes shut. It's impossible. So I turn the TV on and begin watching *World War II in Color*. After one hour, I find myself drifting in and out over the sounds of screaming bombs falling on London. Then my head drops to the side and my eyes shut.

The alarm on my phone goes off loudly on the coffee table. The time is eight in morning. I hear my neck crack as I rotate it. My body aches like I've been hit by a bus. The left side of my face feels sore.

I slowly get up off the couch and go upstairs to wash up. I go back downstairs and make myself a cup of tea and go out to the balcony. I clean up Simone's poop as she does her stretches beside me.

It's a cool morning. I look down at the square and see people going to work. Across the way in the other apartment building I see a man in a gray suit kissing his partner's head goodbye. She's sitting up in bed with her laptop. Pigeons coo below me.

I go back inside and hear the dreadful sound of my phone vibrating on the kitchen counter. I hurry to pick it up. Jack's name appears on the screen.

"So, I did your job, now hand over Jack!" I shout into the phone.

"Good morning to you, Patrick. Isn't it just marvelous outside?" the Bison replies.

"I want to see Jack now!"

"You'll be reunited with Jack very soon. But you must do one more job for me this evening. It's very important you listen, Patrick." I hurry, opening up my fanny pack and removing my notebook and pen. "Keeper Road, six o'clock. You'll meet a man there. He will give you further instructions in what to do. You get all that?"

"Yeah. How do I know you're not going to screw me over?"

"I know I've had you running around the city, but I'm a man of my word. You do this for me, I'll have Jack safe and sound in your embrace. Oh, I nearly forgot, you'll need a driver for this one, good luck."

Fuck!

I slam the phone down on the counter, massaging the middle of my forehead. I'm now getting tension headaches. I remove my hair tie, which helps. I swallow back my last pill.

I fill the dog's bowls with fresh water and food. I scroll through my contacts and call the Bronze Man.

"Hello," I say.

"What's up?"

"The Bison wants me to do one more job this evening at six o'clock on Keeper Road."

"That's good news. I just got in contact with Thomas McCarthy," she says.

"What did he say?"

"He wants to meet in an hour's time at the Garden of Remembrance."

"I'll be there," I reply.

"Are you sure?"

"It's probably not safe for you to be doing this by yourself. I'll see you soon." I hang up the phone and connect the charger to it. I sit at the kitchen counter and start writing in my notebook. I glance up at the fridge. Stuck to it is a photo of me and Olivia in Montenegro, all smiles.

I pick up my phone and text her. *Do you want to drop over Saturday? You left a few things in the loft.* For the first time this week, I get an instant reply from her with the words *Sure, how does two sound?* I reply with a thumbs-up emoji.

TO-DO LIST

GARDEN OF REMEMBRANCE

DOLPHINS BARN

GUN III

SAVE JACK

OLIVIA'S VISIT

CHAPTER THIRTY-FOUR

I begin riding my bike on King Street with my fanny pack strapped around my waist. The sky is the color of sour milk and there's a sharp chill in the air. With one hand, I zip my hoodie all the way up as I pass the Gate Theatre on my left. They're performing Arthur Miller's play *The Price* on stage.

I get off my bike feeling the pain trickle through my body like I've been run over by a bread truck. I lock the bike to a stand. Before I enter the Garden of Remembrance I see the words screwed to a stony wall. They read **DEDICATED TO THOSE WHO GAVE THEIR LIVES IN THE CAUSE OF IRISH FREEDOM.**

In the center of the garden is a crucifix-shaped pool. Inside the pool are beautiful mosaic patterns of broken spears and other weapons. Back in 2011, Queen Elizabeth made a historic visit to Ireland. She laid a wreath and bowed her head in homage to those who fought against her ancestors. I remember the city being shut down for her visit, the paths and roads deserted.

I walk down some steps. The garden is kept spotlessly clean. There's many benches and plants against the wall around the water. As I turn the corner, I see the Bronze Man sitting down smoking a cigar sitting next to Slim, who is wearing his long coat. His lengthy hair is freshly washed and dried.

"Morning," I say to her. I nod to Slim. She's decked out in a short gray jacket with shoulder pads matching her trousers. Underneath is a brown turtleneck jumper and on her feet are off-white New Balance trainers. Her roaring-red hair is tied back in a low bun.

"I could be better, didn't get a wink of sleep last night," she replies. Her eyes are slightly red and bloodshot.

"You do look a bit pale."

"Shut up." She takes a drag of her cigar and shoots out the smoke from her mouth above her head.

"So, where is this Thomas fella?"

"He should be here soon," she says, looking at her yellow-gold Cartier watch. "Are you sure this plan is going to work?"

"We don't have many options."

She looks over my shoulder. "There he is."

Thomas McCarthy is a tall bloke, thick and menacing-looking. His hair is gray but full and his facial hair is in the style of a goatee. He's wearing a tan trench coat.

She looks at Slim. "Keep your distance."

The Bronze Man puts the cigar out in the bin beside her and walks up some steps leading to the sculpture called the *Children of Lir*. I follow her, a few steps behind.

"You got some shiner there," Thomas McCarthy says. "You should put an ice pack on it." He tilts his head and stares at me. "Who's this prick?"

"His name is Patrick," the Bronze Man responds. I count three security men walking about in the garden.

"Why are we meeting? Have you come to confess your sins? I know that one of your men was paid to take out my son." He has a slight underbite when he speaks that shows his stained yellow teeth.

"My men were not involved in the death of your son. I'm not bloody stupid," she says.

He wags his index finger at her. "I heard that you might be shutting down your bar because of a roof misfortune. I think you got desperate, and I have a sneaky suspicion you've been taking on new clients."

"Well, you're wrong," she says. "I'm here to do a deal."

"What kind?"

"Finding your son's killer."

"Sure, I can do that meself. I have a truckload of people doing that right now as we speak," he says. "Why would I have you do it?"

"Patrick here is the best person to do so, that's why."

He smirks at me. "This ol' fella here, no way."

"Trust me, he'll find him fast," she says. "The only thing I want in exchange is my roof to be fixed."

"You're pulling me leg."

"I know the Garda are busy keeping tabs on you and your family, but we can find this prick quickly and most importantly quietly," she says. "Sixty grand and we have a deal."

Thomas snarls and scratches his wrinkled cheek with his long fingernails as we wait for an answer.

"I'm not giving you much time, but if you can find this rat then we have a deal."

The Bronze Man reaches out her hand.

Thomas shakes it but then he pulls her in closely. "But if I find out you're stringing me along or have anything to do with my son's death, I'll make sure you and your crew will be strung up by the neck. Ye hear me?"

He lets go of her hand, pulls up the collar on his trench coat, and walks away.

The Bronze Man looks shaken.

"Find this cunt fast," she says to me and storms off.

~~GARDEN OF REMEMBRANCE~~

CHAPTER THIRTY-FIVE

I ride my bike on Parnell Street, making my way south of the city. The sunlight is desperately trying to penetrate the thick smoky clouds as I reach Cork Street. I turn the handlebars a hard right into the flats. The bike wobbles, making a screeching sound when I go over a small pothole, giving me the butterflies.

When I turn into the estate, I see two Garda vans parked outside Junkie Jake's apartment / drug den. JJ runs a drug den but, just like meself, he has been off the drugs for years now. JJ never sells any drugs but provides sterile needles and syringes.

It sounds mad, but he always says to me, I'd rather the parents did it here in this dump than in front of their children. He says politicians, doctors, and celebrities have shown up at his den.

Tape that reads **GARDA NO ENTRY** surrounds the apartment, located on the ground floor. I get off my bike and push it over, blocked by flapping tape. The sight of flashing blue lights coming from the Garda van is now aggravating me.

There're kids running around, chasing each other, making shrieking sounds like seagulls, and weathered women in bright-colored dressing gowns standing outside, some of them vaping and smoking cigarettes.

I recognize JJ's sister coming out of his apartment and holding her son in her arms. I raise my hand and yell out, "Melissa!"

She sees me and walks over to me. The other day I pointed a SIG Sauer pistol at her son's father, threatening that I would shoot both his kneecaps off and leave him in the wilderness.

"Patrick," she says. Her eyes are soaking wet with tears.

"What happened?"

"JJ has been shot," she says.

"Jesus Christ. Is he alive?"

"Yeah, the last I heard is they took him to St. James's Hospital and removed the bullet from him." Melissa looks devastated as she wipes her wet cheek. I reach into my fanny pack and hand her a tissue. "Thanks." She dabs her face with it. "Who would do such a thing?"

"I was only talking to him the other day, everything seemed all right."

"There was a woman who wasn't so lucky. She was shot in the neck and bled out all over the couch. She was a medical student. Can ye believe it?" I can only shake my head in disbelief. "I'm gonna try to head over later. The Garda were asking me a hundred and one questions earlier."

Her son is playing up in her arms, chewing on the head of a Captain America action figure. "Would ye give it over," she says to the boy, taking the doll from him, then she says to me, "I have to run off."

"I'll drop over to the hospital now," I say.

"You're a saint," she replies, blowing her nose into the tissue.

Just when I'm about to leave I see a stretcher leaving the apartment with a body bag strapped on top. It must be the medical student who was shot.

St. James's Hospital will forever give me the creeps. It's the place where my mother spent her dying months in a coma right up to her final breath. The familiar stuffy odors come rushing back. That nauseating feeling comes over me as I make my way through the hectic emergency room.

A young girl is hunched over, arms folded, rocking back and forth like she has stomach cramps. Beside her is a man in

KEITH BRUTON

construction attire with a bandage around his thumb. His hands are layered in dirt.

I approach the male nurse at the front desk. "I'm looking for my friend Jake, he was brought in earlier. He was shot."

"He's currently recovering in Room 19 on the second floor," he replies.

"Thanks."

I don't have much time to be waiting around in a hospital, but I need to see JJ. I use the stairs to get to the second floor. I see a Garda officer at a vending machine. Shit, I had an idea they would send one to the hospital to keep an eye on JJ. You see it in the movies all the time. The target gets shot but not killed, and later that night the perpetrator sneaks into the hospital to finish the job.

The heavyset officer kneels down and reaches his hand into the vending machine, struggling to find his chocolate bar. With his back to me, I move rapidly and walk into Room 19.

There're four beds in the roasting-hot room, which feels like a sauna. The blinds are fully closed and the room is dark. To my right are two empty beds, which is a rare sight.

A man in his sixties is asleep in the bed to my left, both legs in casts. "Get Well Soon" cards are on top of his bedside table, along with a carton of Quality Street chocolates and a bouquet of blue orchids.

The curtain is fully pulled around the bed beside the injured fella. I walk over and peep through the curtain. I see JJ in the bed, eyes closed. I turn my head to the left and, through the window in the door, see the Garda officer take a seat outside.

I slip through the curtains, closing them behind me. I stand over JJ's bed. An IV drip is inserted in the back of his hand.

I shake his feet, trying to wake the fucker up.

"Wake up," I whisper to him, and I start pinching his big toes.

"What... who's there?" he asks, eyes barely opening.

"It's Patrick, ye eejit," I reply. The heart rate monitor beside him beeps.

"Ah, Patrick. How are things?" he mumbles.

I pull up a chair and sit in front of him. "What happened to ye?"

"With who?" JJ sounds like he's strung out on drugs, which he probably is.

"You, of course. You're after just getting a bullet removed from ye."

"Where am I?"

"Who did this to you?"

JJ licks his dry lips. I grab the plastic cup of water on his bedside table and gently pour it in his mouth. He swallows it back, making a gulping sound. "I don't know... all I remember is a lad in balaclava barging in... he started shooting up the place."

"Jesus. Who would want you dead?"

"I don't bleedin' know."

"Fuck."

"It was all caught on camera," he says.

"What do you mean?"

"I have a camera inside my apartment." He spots his phone on the bedside table and reaches for it. "Me password is six-two-one-four. Click on me security app... " JJ is drifting away on me. "Go to today's date."

I take the phone from him, click on the app, and pull up the video, fast-forwarding to the time of the shooting. I see a man wearing all black barge into JJ's apartment, the door nearly swinging off the hinges. He first shoots JJ in the stomach. JJ falls on the kitchen floor pressing his hand on the wound.

The young medical student is screaming in a frenzy, her mouth wide open. The bloke turns to her and shoots her in the neck. She grabs her neck, choking and bleeding out on the couch. The killer does a runner.

I rewind the video and press play. I pause it and zoom in. I notice something I've seen before. The man is wearing bulky red-and-white Air Jordans.

My heart starts beating faster.

"JJ, does Cracksman Charlie have any relatives in the crime world?" I ask him, but he's nodded off. I nudge him on the shoulder. "Don't fall asleep on me."

"What?" he says, tossing and turning like a dog having a nightmare.

"Does Cracksman Charlie have any relatives in crime?"

"I think he has a brother, but he's in prison, I think."

"What was his name?" He nods off again. I slap JJ on the cheek. "Don't leave me, you fucker, what's his name?"

"The Ro…"

"Come on, for fuck's sake."

"The Rook," he utters. JJ's eyes close.

"Get better soon, ye fool," I whisper to him. He's now in a deep sleep, something I envy.

I sneak out from behind the curtain. The Garda officer is still sitting outside on his phone while eating a Mars bar. Near the toilets I see a wheelchair. I sit down in it and start wheeling out of the room, hoping the officer doesn't stop me.

"Afternoon," I say to him. He has a mouthful of caramel chocolate in his mouth.

"Afternoon," he mumbles back to me.

I wheel myself all the way to the end of the hallway and jump off when I turn the corner. When I get to the elevator, I angrily scribble something off on my do list. I went to JJ's to ask him to be a getaway driver and instead got a name.

"The Rook."

190

CHAPTER THIRTY-SIX

My belly lets out an echoing growl, sounding like an agitated grizzly bear. This fasting business is catching up on me and it's only been a week. All I want to do is eat all day, get fat, and watch old Japanese movies with Olivia in the living room.

The time is edging closer to twelve o'clock, which means I can eat.

I pedal in the tight bike lane on Thomas Street. An electric bike overtakes me, nearly clipping my leg. A rough-looking fella sits down on a bench draining a can of Dutch Gold lager.

The bike rolls down Dame Street, then back uphill, passing a group of backpackers exiting a hostel. Not too far is the Olympia Theatre, which opened 1879. Gladys Knight is in one of the enclosed poster display cases, right next to the musical *Potted Potter*.

Now I can't get the song "License to Kill" by Gladys Knight out of my head. I turn right onto George's Street and lock my bike outside Gino's Gelato.

I see the restaurant. I'm in a hurry to eat." Diwali is an Indian restaurant I've been to a million times. I sit down across from a fish tank built into a wall with a gold frame around it.

Beside a bar filled with wine is a TV showing a Bollywood movie and massive wall art of Indian spices. The lovely waiter comes over with a tall menu. I already know what I'm going to order.

"Chicken tikka masala, basmati rice, naan bread, and a Cobra beer," I say to the short man in a loose-fitting white shirt and black waistcoat.

"Excellent," he replies, snatching the menu from my clammy hands.

I remove my phone from my fanny pack and type in the words *The Rook*. His mug pops up on the first page. I click on one of the few articles written up on him. One of the papers says he was released from prison. The article is six months old. Harry Lynch, aka the Rook, was known to be working with the McCarthys and crime gangs across Europe in the past. Is this the Bison? Is this the man who is behind the kidnapping of Jack and the shooting of JJ?

A round copper dish with my curry arrives along with the steamy basmati rice, hot naan, and beer. He adds another plate to the table. It's popadums with mango chutney and a mint sauce.

I look up at him. "Complimentary," he says.

It all smells delicious. I spend the next ten minutes devouring everything in sight. My belly is heavy with Indian food. I make a phone call, leaning back in the chair and sticking out my stomach like a pregnant lady.

"Hello," I say through the phone, plucking rice from my half-shaven beard.

"Yeah, what's up?" the Bronze Man responds.

"Are you about?"

"I'm just heading into the Dead Zoo."

"Really?"

"I don't want to be near the Crazy Owl, it puts me in a mood."

"I'll be there in ten minutes. Don't move." I hang up the phone and pay the bill, leaving the restaurant a generous tip. I made sure to swallow the rest of my Cobra beer.

I zigzag through town like a MotoGP rider, eventually turning right on Merrion Street Upper. The Department of the Taoiseach (prime minister) is to my left. Some would call the Edwardian building, built between 1904 and 1922, a masterpiece.

Within the monster gates and columns topped with huge urns and statues of Irish scientists William Rowan Hamilton and Robert Boyle is a grand Portland stone palace around a pleasant courtyard. I catch a glimpse of the dome.

The National Museum of Ireland—Natural History, also known as the Dead Zoo, is tucked away next to the government offices. To the right is Leinster Lawn, which is restricted to members of the government.

I lock my bike safely across the road around a bike stand. I enter the peaceful grounds, passing the bronze statue of surgeon Major T. H. Parke guarding the entrance, drenched in sweat, mantled with weaponry. Bird droppings smear his face and rifle like white paint. We have something in common: identical mustaches.

The Dead Zoo building is playing hide-and-seek behind enormous leafy trees. The building is shaped like a long filing cabinet, built in 1856, designed by Frederick Clarendon.

The sign at the entrance reads **FREE ENTRY**. I stroll in.

I haven't been here since my teen years. I would drop in when I would drift around town like an empty fizzy-drink can blowing on the roads, my head in the gray clouds. What am I saying? I still do that.

When I enter, I'm greeted by a massive deer skeleton. Three of them with antlers eight feet wide that would knock you right out cold. I once saw a deer in Phoenix Park shed its antlers, which was a spectacular thing to witness.

I unzip my fanny pack, removing any loose change I have, and slot the coins into the donation box at the front desk. The old security man, who resembles Roald Dahl, smiles and nods at me.

The walls are light yellow, the color of daffodils, and the floors are checkered, black and dark red. Either side of me are glass cases filled with taxidermy, including a golden eagle spreading its wings and a snow leopard lurking, ready to pounce on its prey. Its penetrating blue eyes stare at me as I walk by.

Tall sash windows invite the light in. It shines on a family of badgers and otters. I feel on edge with the dead surrounding me.

All sorts of fishes that swim in the deep blue sea, and birds and mammals that roam the dark forest, are stuffed inside one museum in central Dublin.

I make my way to another open space. A giraffe, hippo, and elephant make me feel miniature, like the group of children in bright-blue school uniforms. They run past me speaking the Irish language, which is refreshing to hear. They are in awe of the basking shark drifting over their tiny heads, hung by the thinnest wires.

I can already see the headline: "PRIMARY SCHOOL CHILDREN CRUSHED BY A STUFFED SHARK."

I walk upstairs to the second floor and get a better view of the museum. I come across an ostrich, a penguin, a giant tortoise, a toucan, and a stingray. I lean over the balcony keeping an eye out for the Bronze Man.

A boy of about eight or so wearing rectangular glasses too big for his face is sitting on a chair not far from me drawing something on a sketch pad. He glances at me, kicking his legs back and forth, then quickly looks back down.

"What ye drawing, young fella?" I ask him, leaning my back into the balcony, arms folded.

"Nothing," he replies timidly, gripping his sketch pad to his chest.

"Go on, show us what you're drawing." My guess is that he drew the skeleton of the humpback whale hanging from the ceiling in front of us. He hands me the sketch pad. I take a look and see a man leaning against a balcony. "Is my nose really that big from the side?"

The boy shrugs his shoulders and smiles.

"Ye did a good job, kid," I say.

"Seamus! What did I tell you about wandering off by yourself?" says a narrow-built woman with tightly coiled hair approaching the boy.

"His sketch is really good," I say to her.

"Yeah, he's a real Michelangelo." She grips the boy by the arm and storms off with him. "Come on, you."

The boy turns his head and sends me a cheeky grin.

I turn around and see the Bronze Man standing in front of me.

"So, this is your place of tranquility," I say to her.

"What's the story?"

We start walking together. "You remember a friend of mine called JJ?"

"I can't recall," she says as we pass some stuffed puffins.

"He's after getting shot."

"Did he survive?"

"Yeah, he's recovering in St. James's Hospital." I remove my phone from my fanny pack. "Do you know this man?" I ask, showing her a photo of the Rook. She gives me one of those pale, worrisome expressions.

"I knew this would come back to haunt me. This is the man who organized the hit of William Hughes. He worked for the McCarthys at the time."

"Worked?"

"Until the McCarthys made him take the fall on possession of heroin. It wasn't much but it was enough to put him behind bars for three years."

"Jesus Christ. I think he's responsible for shooting JJ and the kidnapping of Jack Magee. I think he knows we're inching closer to him. But why use me to do all his dirty work?"

"I never told the Rook about you, but word does get around," she says. "He's a smart fella but not a killer."

"Something doesn't add up," I say. "The Rook got help from someone. Two men kidnapped Jack. I thought it would be his brother Cracksman Charlie, but the Bison has a very distinctive voice on the phone." We both stop walking. We can hear two kids chasing each other below.

"The night you murdered William Hughes, it was game, set, match. The whole Hughes family crumbled like a granny falling on a frosty morning. They either got arrested or fled the country. The McCarthys took over everything and they've been growing ever since."

"Did William Hughes have children?"

"John Hughes was his only child, but he's locked up in prison now," she says.

I hear the floorboards creak behind us. Caitríona is walking toward us with her dog, Bowie, in a bag. His head is sticking out from it. He's still wearing the cone like a lampshade.

"How are things?" she asks.

"You can't bring dogs in here," the Bronze Man says.

"Says bloody who?"

"I need a getaway driver," I tell the Bronze Man. "With JJ in the hospital, I have no other options."

"I can do that, I'm an excellent driver," Caitríona says confidently, chin raised high.

"No, no," the Bronze Man replies. "It might be dangerous."

"So bleedin' what? I need something dangerous in my life, it's getting a bit stale working for you."

The Bronze Man looks at me for approval.

"Meet me in Smithfield Square at five o'clock," I say to Caitríona. She makes a tight fist, lifting the bag high in the air. The dog lets out a high-pitched bark.

"Can't wait," she says, smiling. "What is that? It smells like curry in here."

CHAPTER THIRTY-SEVEN

Two o'clock. I don't have much time. The thought of asking Eagle Eye for a gun again makes me wince, so I decide to go elsewhere. From the Dead Zoo on Merrion Street Upper, I head southwest, cycling on St. Stephen's Green, listening to a cover version of "Helter Skelter" by Mötley Crüe.

I turn left on Wexford Street, which is pulsating with pedestrians and traffic. I finally slither my way up on the path and reach Pleasants Street. I see a woman hitting the seventy mark standing outside the bike shop talking to a thin, baby-faced Garda officer.

"What seems to be problem, Officer?" I ask him.

"Do you work here?"

"Yeah."

"Do you know where Jack Magee might happen to be?" he asks with pen and notebook in hand. The attractive woman has white veneers on full display and makeup on.

"He had a family emergency to attend to in the country," I say.

"Really? He never contacted me about a family emergency," she says. "I was supposed to see him a few days ago and he never replied. I've been calling and texting him nonstop."

"I was on the phone to him yesterday… said he lost his phone. He has habit of losing things."

The Garda closes his notebook.

"So, he's safe and sound?" the Garda asks, like the woman wasted his time. I give him a reassuring nod. "Great news. See, everything is just fine, Mrs. Flack," he says and gets into his vehicle.

"So, Jack is okay?" she asks me.

"Yeah, the last time I spoke to him. You must be the florist from down the road. He said some nice things about you."

"My niece begs to differ. She said I've been *ghosted*, whatever that means." She fiddles with her necklace. "You wouldn't happen to know what kind of family emergency it would be?"

"I think he said an uncle from England."

"He must be very old."

"Very, very old," I say.

"Do you know when he'll be back?"

"Haven't a clue, but I reckon he'll be back soon, it doesn't look too well for this uncle of his."

"Oh my," she says. "How awful."

"I'll make sure he contacts you when he's gets back."

"You're a good lad," she says, all cheerful. "I'm not giving up on him just yet."

I push through the door of the bike shop. I walk over to Jack's workstation. His desk is full of crap. I pull on the drawer and find what I'm looking for. I open up his journal and turn the pages. Halfway into the journal I land on a page with a phone number scribbled on top and a list of names:

The Golden Boy
The Swiss Maestro
Black Mamba
The Greatest
Lightning Bolt
The Bambino

The only name I recognize on the page is the Black Mamba, and what the bloke handed me at the Hungry Tree, a tranquilizer gun. These names could mean bloody anything.

Lightning Bolt could be a feckin' Taser gun. I know Muhammad Ali was called the Greatest and Maradona was nicknamed the Golden Boy. Does that mean the weapon is going to be small and nippy like a grenade? I can't be running around the city with a bloody grenade.

And the Bambino, which Babe Ruth was dubbed, is going to be big like a bazooka? Or maybe simply a baseball bat. I can't be going into war with a baseball bat.

Jack put in his order over the phone, so this was really my only chance. I call the number.

The phone rings out.

"Yes," answers a woman, her voice soft, tender, like I've rung up a twenty-four-hour crisis helpline and she's ready to listen to all my darkest secrets. I scramble for a reply.

"I would like the Swiss Maestro," I respond, not knowing what I ordered, but it sounds like a fancy cheese.

"The Famine Memorial in one hour, bring a grand," she instructs me.

"One h—"

The phone line goes dead. The call is over and I need to get a move on and collect my weapon. The sunlight shines into my eyes through the top window above the main entrance.

I look around the bike shop. It's so still. For a second or two I get a nauseating feeling in the pit of my stomach like a wave has swept me back into the sea.

I get back on my bike and cycle north. The gray paths have these perfect raindrops shaped like spots you would see in a Damien Hirst painting. I feel the drops bounce off my hands as I turn the handlebars right on Hatch Street Upper. I get off my bike and rush to an ATM, removing eight hundred euro. I already have two hundred euro in me fanny pack.

I've got a grand cash on me now.

I ride my bike hurriedly, out of breath, arriving on the quays with my T-shirt stuck to my back. I'm now dripping and my body is aching. I make my way over the Seán O'Casey Bridge, dodging a few pedestrians. I jump off my bike and push it slowly toward the Famine Memorial. I lock it to a railing overlooking the Liffey.

The winds are picking up and the water below is vicious. The gulls are out doing their usual rounds of being noisy cunts and causing havoc to the city. I'm now in the financial district.

The buildings to my left are in the shape of a pyramid and to my right is the Liberty Hall, which is one of Dublin's tallest buildings.

As I approach the Famine Memorial, I get the shivers. The view is magnificent. "La mamma morta" by Maria Callas should really be playing as I approach the haunting group of statues representing the hardship and pain caused by the failure of the potato crop during the 1840s.

The gaunt figures are like something out of *The Walking Dead*, barefoot and wearing ragged clothing, clutching onto their belongings. One of them carries a child on their shoulders as a timid dog follows behind the group. I'm in the depths of hell.

"We meet again," says a man sitting on a bench. When I get a closer look, it's the same bloke from last weekend who I met at the Hungry Tree in King's Inns Park.

He's wearing black boots instead of chestnut shoes, navy-blue jeans instead of tight black jeans, and a black denim jacket, buttoned up. I sit next to him.

"Miserable fuckin' day," he says.

"That's Dublin for ye."

"It's all bollocks."

"You should consider moving abroad," I say.

"I was actually thinking that. Aren't people buying apartments in Spain all the time?"

"Or you could rent, it's cheaper than here." I slide the envelope with the money onto the bench between us. He quickly takes the envelope and does the switch with an envelope of his own. I take it.

"Anywhere is fuckin' cheaper than here. You would think it's London with the cost of property… it's all bad."

There's a moment of silence as he stares out at the Liffey.

All you can hear are seagulls squawking and squealing. And the strong gusts of wind push the Liffey into Dublin Bay.

"I saw a penguin kill itself," he says out of nowhere, shaking his head. "Waddling off straight toward the mountains, away from its colony and the water… to its certain doom. The camera operator who was filming the penguin was blown away. I haven't really gotten over it." I didn't have a response for him. I just sat and waited. "I better be going." He stands up.

"The Swiss Maestro is named after someone, who?" I ask.

"The great Roger Federer, of course."

"It's not a tennis racket, so what's inside?"

"I don't want to ruin the surprise," he says with a sneaky smile, walking away.

~~GUN III~~

CHAPTER THIRTY-EIGHT

The dark gray clouds in the sky are monstrous, filthy and violent. My phone reads a smidgen after three as a fat raindrop falls on my screen. I needed to stop all this prancing about like a fuckin' tap dancer and get a move on.

I pedal back to Smithfield feeling my calves tense up and harden. I rush into my apartment complex before the showers come pouring down to drench me. The sensation of wet clothing stuck to my body makes me quiver, right up there with getting sand in your shoes after a long walk on the beach.

I arrive inside my stuffy loft with my bike. Simone runs over to welcome me. She's full of energy, which I cannot match at this moment in time.

"How are you, missy?" I say, patting her head. I lean my bike against the wall and remove my fanny pack from my waist, dumping it on the kitchen counter. I'm very curious to see what is inside the package the peculiar fellow handed me on the Liffey. His talking about penguins killing themselves was a real downer.

I rip open the envelope with my teeth and slide the object out onto the kitchen counter. I pick the object up. "So, this is the Swiss Maestro."

I'm holding a Luger pistol. The thing looks like an antique, something the Germans might have used in World Wars I and II.

I aim the gun at the fridge. The pistol features wooden grips, blued finish on the barrel and frame, and brass finish on the trigger, takedown pins, and safety lever.

It feels dainty.

Simone glances up at me, waving her tail. She jumps on my thigh, arching her back, digging her paws and sharp nails into my skin.

The pistol has an eight-round capacity and is ready for action. I leave the gun on the kitchen counter. My stomach feels swollen after the curry from earlier. I dunk my head into the freezer, letting the cold air hit my sore face.

I grab a frozen bag of sliced bananas and strawberries. I cut the bag open with a knife and dump the fruit in a blender, adding Greek yogurt, milk, and a tiny spoonful of peanut butter.

I turn on the blender, which makes a distressing sound Simone detests. She starts barking and running around in circles like she does when I point the hair dryer at her.

I remove a stainless-steel straw from the drawer and start sucking up the thick smoothie. The cold hurts my teeth but I fight through the pain. I refill Simone's bowl with fresh water and place a couple of doggy treats in the other bowl.

I run back upstairs to the bedroom and change into clean clothing, all black. I check the weather on my phone for the rest of the evening: most of Dublin will be dry and very mild with a mix of cloud and hazy sunshine. Thicker clouds will, however, bring patchy outbreaks of drizzle later tonight.

I make sure my phone is fully charged and I have everything I need for tonight's mission. The time is closing in on five o'clock. Something doesn't smell right in the bedroom. The pungent odor is familiar as I look around on the floors.

In the corner I see the damage.

"Simone, ye dirty bitch!" She's been pooing everywhere. I see Simone sitting at the bottom of the stairs staring up at me. "Bold girl," I shout down at her, wagging my finger.

I quickly clean up the mess with a tissue. The dog hovers at my feet with sorrow. It's not too long before I give in to her big brown eyes. I pet her down one last time. "I'll see you later, okay?" I say, kissing the top of her head.

My phone lets out a buzzing sound on the coffee table like an annoying housefly. I pick it up. A text from Caitríona, which reads *Outside loser.*

This evening I'm leaving without my bike, which feels foreign. The fanny pack is strapped around my waist, and inside it are my leather gloves, keys, face mask, phone, cash, and Luger pistol. I'm ready.

When I get outside I see Caitríona pull up in her black-and-white Smart Forfour coupe.

I open up the passenger's door.

"You can't be serious," I say to her.

"What's wrong?"

"I thought you were going to show up in a bigger car. Not this bloody thing."

"It's the perfect vehicle. It's like the movie *The Italian Job*, except we're in a Smart car and not a Mini," she says in her black leather jacket.

"The one with Michael Caine?" I respond, stepping into the car.

"No, the one with Mark Wahlberg and Charlize Theron. She's a little ride, isn't she?"

"Why is everyone I know in my life not fully right in the head?" I put my seat belt on.

"Have you seen yourself in the mirror?" she replies. I catch a glimpse of my botched beard job in the rearview mirror. She isn't wrong.

"Keeper Road," I instruct her.

The sun is out and the roads and paths are glistening with deep puddles. The tiny car swerves left on Queen Street, where traffic is dismal, making me want to vomit. I pull the window down on my side for some air.

Caitríona is rapping to "The Magic Number" by De La Soul playing on the stereo.

I turn down the volume. "If this job doesn't go according to plan, I want you to leave."

"Why?"

"Just do it. I don't want you mixed up in it. You get the fuck out of there and burn this vehicle, along with your clothing, far away from the city. And destroy your SIM card."

She rolls up her sleeves, revealing the head of the grasshopper tattoo on her forearm. "I won't need to burn the vehicle. The license plates are fake and the minute this is over I'm sending the car to the garage for a spray-paint and new wheels. It's going to look like a brand-new fuckin' car when it's all done."

We turn left on Herberton Road, then cross a teeny bridge that I could do a long jump over. I stare out the window at the clouds, which resemble perfect brushstrokes by the hand of Gerhard Richter.

"Getting close." Caitríona turns off the stereo as we make a right. We slowly approach an industrial estate made up of many large steel buildings. "This must be it."

"Park in front of the skip over there," I say, pointing.

Caitríona parks the car. The yellow skip in front of us has a mountain full of crap, including a cracked bathtub, a rusty basin, a shattered mirror, and hundreds of broken tiles. I remember when I was younger I would see these things up in flames in someone's front garden. Occasionally you still see this happening. Troubled teens have nothing better to do than steal cars, burn skips, and smash windows of derelict buildings, causing mayhem.

I put on my leather gloves. "I want you to stay in the car and make sure you're ready when we come out."

"Do you know what the job is?"

"No, but I reckon it'll get a bit hairy inside and you might need to do a legger, ye hear me?"

"How long do you want me to hang around?"

"Twenty minutes. If I'm not out by then, leave."

A knock comes hurtling on the back window. I see a bloke wearing all black and a face mask standing near the car. I roll the window all the way down.

"Open up," he says.

I nod to Caitríona.

The bloke sits in the back seat. We both turn around, facing the man in black. "Here's what's happening. The McCarthys and the Polish are doing an exchange in that warehouse across the way," the bloke says, pointing with his finger.

"What kind of exchange?" I ask.

"Guns and money. The McCarthys are handing over one million in cash to the Polish. Both gangs will have five people each in the exchange. Our objective is to get inside and get a hold of the bag full of cash."

"Ye can't be serious," I say.

"I'm dead fuckin' serious."

Caitríona has a troubling look on her face like the blood has been drained from her.

"And when this is done, you take me to Jack?" I ask.

"Exactly, once we have the money I'll take you right to Jack," the bloke says. "Do you have a gun on ye?"

"Yeah."

"Good. Here they come now," he says as a red van turns into the warehouse, followed by an olive-green Mercedes-Benz that looks like it belongs in an African safari. He pulls out a gas mask from his backpack. "Put this on."

"Why do we need this?" I ask as he hands it to me.

"I'm going to toss a tear gas grenade into the warehouse. It will disorientate the lot of them, giving us a better chance of getting a hold of the money."

We both put the gas masks on. We look like something out of *Breaking Bad*. I find it difficult to breathe in it. My chest already feels heavy and my face is warming up. "You just be ready, missy, when we come out," he says to Caitríona. "Here's the McCarthy gang now."

A silver Mitsubishi Outlander turns into the warehouse and parks outside. Five rugged-looking men step out of it and go inside. One of them is carrying a gym bag.

"Let's go!" the bloke says.

We jump out of the tiny vehicle and run across the road. The area is dead.

"Follow me." The bloke pulls out a Springfield Armory XD pistol from his trousers. I reach into my fanny pack and briskly remove the Swiss Luger. "We need to get to the top of those stairs."

We run up the outdoor staircase, leading to a door. I hear footsteps beyond it.

"Wait!" I shout with my hand up, feeling my warm breath on my face.

The door slowly opens. A man wearing a bomber jacket is standing in front of us with a priceless expression on his face.

I run up the steps and stop the man from reaching for his gun, while the bloke knocks him over the head with his weapon.

The man drops to the ground, landing between us.

The bloke nods to go inside. The lighting is poor and I feel claustrophobic in the mask. We kneel down on the metal flooring, edging closer to the railing, peeking over.

The red van is parked in the middle of the warehouse. The two gangs are facing each other in straight lines like they are about to perform an Irish dance. My mask starts to steam up from my heavy breathing.

"Everything is here," says a skinhead with a dark beard and a nasty scar on the side of his face. The back doors to the van open wide. The skinhead unzips three large bags. "These are the best guns to come into your country."

From my position, I can see handguns and boxes of ammo.

One member of the McCarthy gang, a man wearing a green blazer like something that gets thrown on the winner of the Masters at Augusta National Golf Club, examines the guns.

"They're good," Green Blazer says to another fella in a long-sleeve white shirt.

I look over beside me and see the bloke, who now has a tear gas grenade in his hand. It's all about to begin and I'm starting to sweat.

"Ready." The bloke pulls on the ring, raising his arm high before releasing the grenade over the balcony railing. I watch it in slow motion bounce on the floor between the two gangs. "Go! Go! Go!"

The white fumes fill up the warehouse in no time. The two gangs start coughing, shouting and waving their hands in the air. We run down the steps. The bloke starts shooting at the gangs, striking one of them in the back.

I can't see shit. The skinhead comes running toward me, blindly throwing punches, coughing uncontrollably. I grab him by the arm and shoot him in the thigh. He buckles to the floor screaming, eyes piercing red as if they are going explode from his eye sockets. Mucus is pouring from his nose as he crawls for my feet like a zombie.

My partner in crime starts shooting into the crowd of wailing men, not seeing a thing. Bodies are dropping left, right, and center. One of the men picks up the bag of money.

"He's getting away with the money," the bloke yells through the mask.

I hear gunshots going off. A bullet knocks out a light fixture, making it go dark inside. The lingering fumes make it impossible to see clearly. Disorientated, I maneuver my way around the warehouse looking for the bag. Then I feel someone kick me in the back. I dive forward on the floor, the pistol slipping from my gloved hand.

The bloke shoots Green Blazer in the shoulder. Green Blazer limps over to the exit door and opens it up, letting the sunlight in and the white fumes spill out.

I look for my gun on the floor. I see it under the wheel of the van. I reach for it, feeling like I'm in a bleedin' video game. I hear the red van starting up. I snatch the pistol. The van reverses, nearly running over my hand.

The van roars, crashing into a tall metal column. Guns fall out the back of the van as sharp broken glass sprays out on the floor. The driver is knocked out cold, smothered by the steering wheel airbag. The white fumes are thinning out as I stand up and look for the man with the bag of money.

"Over there," I yell out.

The bloke and I corner the fella who's holding the bag. Everybody else has left the building. The disgruntled fella shoots at me with a Beretta M9, missing me by three feet.

The bloke and I both shoot at the same time, striking the fella in stomach, chest, leg, and head. The gunshots are loud inside the warehouse, sounding like rapid thunder. Bullet shells soar up in the air beside me.

My shots are more accurate, deadly, unlike the bloke's in the gas mask.

The bag lies next to the dead man. I walk over and pick it up by the handles.

"Let's get the fuck out of here!" the bloke says. We both run out of the warehouse, fast on our feet. It's a mad scene. Two men running around on the streets of Dublin in gas masks. We jump into the tiny car, slamming the doors.

"Go!" I yell to Caitríona. The wheels of the Smart car make a screeching sound on the road as we make our way through the neighborhood. Sweat rolls down my neck into my shirt.

"Where we going?" Caitríona shouts anxiously.

"Turn left up here," says the bloke in the back seat. "Park outside the main entrance of the church over there."

Caitríona presses on the brakes.

"Now, hand over the bag," the bloke says to me.

"Not until I have Jack," I say.

"Hand it fuckin' over now before I put a bullet in that thick skull of yours." He presses the muzzle of his gun against my temple.

As I'm about to hand over the bag, Caitríona pushes down on the accelerator and the bloke falls back. I jump in the back seat and grab him by the forearm, lifting his hand up. He pulls the trigger, blasting two bullets out the windshield.

Caitríona swerves left and right on the road, colliding with parked cars.

"Give me the fuckin' money!" he shouts again as we wrestle in the back seat.

I grip his arm tight and start shaking him viciously. The gun flings out of his hand onto the front passenger seat. He elbows me in the neck. The mask is suffocating my face. I can't see anything through the foggy lens.

He stretches out his arm, reaching for the gun, then suddenly Caitríona grabs it and pushes down on the brake, making the bloke fall forward. She aims the gun and shoots him in the side of the head. Blood is propelled everywhere, including the windshield.

Out of fuckin' breath, I remove my mask, which is drenched in fluids. I feel like passing out in the back seat.

I glance up at Caitríona, who has splattered blood all over her face like she fell into a redberry pie. She wipes her lips with her fingertips.

"You okay?" I ask her.

"Yes... I'm good, but now I'm really going to have to set this car on fire."

I lift the gas mask off the bloke. The Rook's face appears, but who is he working for?

I remove my phone from my fanny pack and dial Jack's number. I wait a few seconds, my head beating like I'm running a marathon, but I'm nowhere near the finish line.

"Hello," the Bison says on the other end.

"Your mate fell into a bit of trouble. Shot dead," I say. "It doesn't look pretty."

"That's a shame," he says.

"It's not all doom and gloom. I have the bag of money if you still want to hand over Jack."

"I'm at Royal Hospital Kilmainham." The Bison hangs up before I can say anything else.

Caitríona is trying to wipe the blood off the windshield, but it keeps getting worse through all the smearing. The two bullet holes above resemble a bloody smiley face.

The Rook's body lies between the two front seats. I pull his body into the back seat, laying him down on his side. "Take me to Kilmainham." She doesn't respond. "Caitríona!"

She turns her head toward me, somewhat dazed. "Yeah?"

"We need to get a move on," I say.

"I really shouldn't be driving around in this thing," she says.

I look at the Rook's dead body and back at Caitríona. "Your first kill?"

She nods while gripping the steering wheel.

"Just remember he could have killed us both... The job isn't over yet."

Caitríona starts up the car and gets a move on. We drive on Slievenamon Road, making a right on Suir Road, hoping nobody spots us and that we don't find ourselves bumping into the Garda.

Once we drive over the bridge and make a dodgy right on Kilmainham Lane, I can see the gray stone walls that surround the iconic landmark.

"Turn left up here," I say.

The banged-up car turns into the grounds. The hilly path leads all the way up to the oldest classical building in Ireland, the Royal Hospital Kilmainham, built in 1680 and based on Les Invalides in Paris.

"That will do," I say. "Get out of here and burn everything."

"I'll see you soon," she responds, her poor face tarnished with blood.

CHAPTER THIRTY-NINE

I grab the bag of money, slam the door shut, and begin walking toward the historic building. The grounds are silent, except for the sounds of birds hiding in the trees, watching me.

The North Wing contains the Master's Quarters, the Great Hall, the Chapel, the Vaulted Cellars, and the kitchen, while the South, East, and West Wings originally provided accommodation for pensioners. Now they're used as museum spaces.

The main entrance door is unlocked. I walk in, pulling my Swiss Luger pistol from my fanny pack. It feels like I've gone back in time. Like I'm in a war and I've split from my platoon in France.

I gradually take my time skimming the hallway. I push another door to my right. When I enter, I see a puddle of dark blood on the marble floor. I get closer and find a body. It's a security woman in her sixties with her back against the wall. Her uniform is soaked in blood.

She's been shot three times. Two in the stomach and one in the head. The tall sash window above her has a spiderweb crack in it from a bullet. A sloppy kill.

Gripping the pistol, I step through another door and come to the majestic courtyard paved in cobblestones. The clock tower is high up to my left, casting its shadow down upon me. The sunlight shines vibrantly on the courtyard, making it even more pleasing to the eye, reminding me of Piazza San Marco in Venice.

I hear the sound of a whining door swinging open from the corner of the courtyard, then the sound of squealing wheels on the ground. Out from the shadows I see Jack. A rope similar to what a climber would use is squeezing his body tightly in the wheelchair, his mouth is gagged with duct tape, and his face is bloodstained and bruised.

The man pushing him turns the wheelchair, halts, and faces him toward me.

"John Hughes, aka the Bison," I say. "The son of William Hughes. I should have known you were the snake behind all this."

"You were getting close, I'll give ye that." He's wearing black jeans and a white polo shirt. I can see a bison tattooed on his thick forearm from where I'm standing. He has a menacing expression on his face.

"I have your m—"

"You murdered my fuckin' family! It's because of you everything went down the drain," he shouts back at me, his teeth flaring fiercely.

"I was doing my job. If it wasn't me, it would have been somebody else that took your father out, and deep down, you know it. You got what you wanted in the end. Lorcan Doyle, Dylan McCarthy, and the money." I hold up the gym bag high. "You can now ride into the bleedin' sunset with your million."

There's a nervy silence between us.

"I'm a man of my word," the Bison says. "Hand over the bag." I throw it over to him. He catches it with both hands. He unzips it and takes a look inside. "With Lorcan Doyle and the son dead…things will be very different with the McCarthys. However, we have one slight problem."

"What's that?"

"The Rook didn't come back with you, and some people mightn't be too happy."

When the Bison finishes his sentence, I hear a thundering bang and feel something graze my right calf. I fall on my knee and look around in a panic. I see a figure to my right. I shoot back with the Luger pistol. I limp for cover behind a column in the cool shade. Blood is running down my leg.

"Come out, ye little rat!" a voice bellows. I catch a glimpse of Cracksman Charlie holding a Glock 17. Another bullet fires my way, striking a glass door, shattering it to pieces. The shots are viciously loud. "You killed my brother! Come out now!"

I see the Bison doing a runner with the bag of money. Jack is left hopelessly in the wheelchair. I jump behind another column as more bullets come spraying in.

Cracksman Charlie stands in the middle of the place like a bleedin' head case. I can't waste any more time. The rounds of bullets come again. I peek out and see him reloading. It's my chance.

I limp quickly toward him as he struggles to load his magazine in time. I shoot him in the chest and again in the throat. He drops to the ground pressing on the wound, trying to stop the blood from spilling out. I stand over him and put the final bullet in his head. The pool of blood is staining the cobblestones.

I pick up the Glock 17 beside him and limp over to Jack to remove the tape from his mouth and untie the ropes around his wrists and ankles.

"I'll be back in minute, Jack," I say to him.

"Kill the bastard!" he utters at me, losing his breath.

I sluggishly jog off out into the enchanting gardens with perfectly trimmed hedges and grass cut in stripe patterns. The sun is beaming down on my face and my calf is killing me. I'm sweating all over my body. I see my prey in the distance galloping away like a gazelle.

"John Hughes! John Hughes!" The scream cuts up my dry throat.

He turns around holding the bag of money by the handles. I trickle down the steps in front of me. We lock eyes like two rams about to bash their horns against each other. I inch closer to him until I'm twenty feet away.

"Have you not done enough killing for today?" he shouts at me. He's a large man with bulging shoulders and a thick neck.

"I still got one job to do," I reply to him, holding the gun in my hand.

"If this is how it's going to end... then no guns." He slowly reaches for his gun in his back pocket, throws it on the stones, and smiles with his arms out wide, inviting me into a fist fight.

My body is in a jock. Why would I want to do that? So, I shoot him three times in the chest. He drops to the ground. I slowly walk over to his body and look down at him on his back. The Bison is dead.

I unzip my fanny pack and remove my phone.

"Tell Thomas McCarthy to come down to the Royal Hospital Kilmainham now," I say to the Bronze Man.

"Did you find him?" I don't respond. I see Jack hobbling down the steps in front of me. I limp my way over to him. Both of us are wounded soldiers. All I want to do is hug him tight and that's what I do.

"They could never break us," he says into my ear.

I send Jack home in a taxi. He needs time to recover. Within twenty minutes, the McCarthy gang shows up and begins cleaning up the mess I've just made. Blokes wearing rubber gloves pick up bullet shells and guns and scrub the blood up in the courtyard and in the gardens.

The Bronze Man is standing next to me in an oversize beige bomber jacket with the scent of citrus perfume and smoky cigars.

"What a fuckin' shit show," she says as Thomas McCarthy comes walking over to us, glistening in sweat, holding his trench coat over his arm.

"How this prick slipped through my fingers is beyond me." He stares down at the Bison's dead body, his white polo shirt soaked in blood. "We had eyes on him the minute he got out of prison."

"That's because the Rook and Cracksman Charlie were doing his dirty work." I remove my clammy gloves.

"I didn't think Cracksman Charlie would have it in him to try a stunt like this. The Rook and John must have planned this out for months, when they were both locked up." The sun is still out and strong. He wipes his forehead with a handkerchief. "How did you know it was these fools all along?"

"A contact of mine told me about Cracksman Charlie and how he might have information on the murder of your son, but something was off when I met him," I say. "He seemed to know more than he was letting on. I followed his brother, the Rook, until he ended up at a warehouse on Keeper Road. I took out the Rook, which led me here."

"So, that's who fucked my deal. Rats everywhere I look these days, ye can't fuckin' move without getting bitten." He nods to one of the young fellas cleaning up. The fella brings the bag of cash over to him. McCarthy gives the Bronze Man a bundle of cash. "Here's payment for your roof and for the job. I would have preferred to have got me fuckin' hands on John meself. There's a lot more in it, if ye come work for me. I don't need an answer now. Sleep on it."

He puts his trench coat back on, adjusts his collar, then takes in a deep breath. "Now it's time to bury me son."

~~SAVE JACK~~

CHAPTER FORTY

The next day, I wake up at twelve. It was one of the better sleeps I've had this month. The sun is spewing through the loft windows like the dome of St. Peter's Basilica.

The bandage around my calf has dry blood on it. My face and body ache but I should be fully recovered in a week or two. Nothing a few ice baths can't fix.

This whole week has been utter madness. So many lives have been taken.

I dump out all my clothing from last night's war in the bin. I have a long shower and trim my beard evenly. I dry my body and hair, lotion up, brush my teeth, and spray two squirts of pungent cologne on my neck before I put on fresh clothing.

I drop an electrolyte tablet into a pint of water and watch it dissolve before I drink it. I take my vitamins and begin making a grilled ham-and-cheese sandwich with a cup of tea.

After breakfast, I give Nocturnal a quick ring. The phone call doesn't last long, but I do fill him in on the details of what happened yesterday evening, obviously leaving out my involvement. I say that this John Hughes fella was to blame for the death of Lorcan Doyle and that he tried to take down the McCarthys' drug operation.

Nocturnal is a bright fella and probably knows I had something to do with it. However, he seems to be happy with the hot gossip before the news outlets get their hands on it. His last response to me is, "See you in the near future, Patrick."

Once Simone is fed, I get her leash and head out the door with her. She's in better spirits today, like she knows I'm more relaxed.

I walk on the quays, breathing in the fresh Dublin air. The streets are nice and quiet for some reason, which I love. It means I can cut through Grafton Street without any hassle.

There's a young girl in wide-leg trousers and a fishnet vest playing Bach on a Yamaha piano. I take a moment to listen and unwind for the first time this week.

I walk the dog to St. Stephen's Green before cutting down onto Camden Street. I eventually make it to Pleasants Street. Simone runs into the bike shop and launches herself on Jack. He has a plaster on the side of his face and his eyebrow has a nasty bruise.

"Simone... how is me sweetheart," he says, rubbing her flappy ears. Simone starts licking his face. "Give it over, now."

"How are you keeping?"

"It's like nothing happened." He leans back in his swivel chair. "But I'm going to have to put more security cameras up and an emergency lock on the door."

"You should really think of retiring."

"Why would I do that, now?"

"Wouldn't you rather be on a beach somewhere warm?"

"I hate the sand," he says. "And you know that."

"What about a cabin in the woods?"

"All alone with my thoughts, are you mad? I need to be in the city where I'm alive," he says. "Why do you want me to retire? Is it because I got taken away by those rats?"

"Well, it was my fault, wasn't it?"

"It wasn't your doing. I should have reached for my gun in the drawer," he says, pulling on the handle and seeing the drawer empty. "Where the hell is it?"

"Sorry, I had to borrow it."

"Do you still have it?"

"You could try searching for it in the Dodder."

"I liked that gun very much." He slams the drawer shut.

"I used your contact from your journal," I say. "The bloke I met up with isn't all there in the head."

"Dermot? He's harmless…worked in the Irish Army for years. I think he saw a few unsavory things on duty with the UN in the Middle East and Africa."

"You should really get some rest."

"I slept like a baby last night, I'm brand-spanking-new."

"I talked to the flower lady yesterday."

"I totally forgot about her. What did she say to ye?"

"She was very worried about your disappearance," I say. "She thought you ghosted her. I said you had a family emergency to attend and that your phone was broken…Nice lady."

"She is, she is. I'll make sure to see her sometime today."

"I need to head… Try get some more rest, ye hear me?" I say, tilting my head and staring at him.

"What are you, my mother?" he replies, struggling to get up out of the chair. "Now, get a move on before I kick you out."

I wave goodbye to Jack. I put my sunglasses on and begin walking toward Cuffe Street. My phone vibrates. I answer it.

"Hello."

"Get your arse down to Mary's Lane," Eagle Eye says.

"Why?"

"Trust me. I think you'll like what I'm about to show ye," he says. I can hear the slyness slip from his lips.

"Okay, give me twenty minutes, the dog's after pooping all over the path." Simone leaves a handful on the sidewalk. I scoop it up with one of those biodegradable poop bags and throw it in the bin, which is full to the rim.

She has bundles of energy this morning. She yanks her neck forward like one of the greyhounds I saw a few days ago. Up ahead, children are playing football on artificial grass and tourists are rolling suitcases into a triangular-designed hotel. A walking tour gathers around the bronze statue of one of Ireland's greatest folk singers, Luke Kelly.

We make it to Mary's Lane earlier than expected.

The Victorian redbrick building is to our right. I walk to one of the entrances. The doors are locked. I go to the other side of the building. Simone is sniffing the dirty paths. Rubbish is on the ground like it's the aftermath of a music festival.

There are stunning paneled timber doors with cast iron at the corner in a round arch. The Dublin insignia of three castles is above the doors. Slightly above that, there's a head sculpted from stone with a dead smile on its face. One door is ajar. Simone pushes the door with her paw. I hear it scratch the surface. I close the door behind me.

It's dark inside. Lingering in the air is the vile smell of dead fish. The sunlight casts shadows of the cast-iron gates. It feels like we've been taken back a hundred years.

I hear the dog breathing heavily. Weeds grow out between the cracks in the floor. It's like a forest when we get deeper. Abandoned. The building forgotten. All sorts of greenery cover the walls, windows, and balconies.

"Up here," I hear a voice yell out.

"What the f—"

"To your left, ye gobshite." I look up and see Eagle Eye hiding in the shadows. He takes a hit of his vape pen, blowing the smoke out from the side of his mouth. "Come up."

I let the dog off the leash. She legs it off, sniffing around, her tail swinging about in excitement. I walk up some dodgy stairs. They shake and make a screeching sound.

"Why did you call me … ? Don't you know it's my rest day?" I say to him.

"Do you have somewhere important to be?"

"You really are testing my patience."

"Relax, I have a present for you."

"What are you talking about?"

Eagle Eye takes a few steps backward, turns around, and removes a white sheet from something large. "Isn't it a fine thing," he says, eyes glowing.

Underneath the sheet is a Barrett M82 sniper rifle.

"It's stunning." I run my hand along the barrel.

"That's not the best part," he says. "I heard you ran into some trouble last week on a job," he says. "I saw the video of you squirming around in an octagon cage. Sammy turned you into a right pretzel."

"That video doesn't show the whole fight."

"It's okay, we all make mistakes, don't we? Sure, I owe you after that mess I made with those pedos out in Dunsink."

"I suppose," I say. "I'm just not in the mood to play games."

"I know, I know, but this is going to be fun."

Eagle Eye skips over to the wall with the vape pen dangling from his lips and flicks a switch inside a fuse box. The lights turn on. I look over the rusty balcony. Below, I see a man in just his underwear, blindfolded and tied to a wooden board. I can see the sweat sliding down his chest from where I'm standing.

"Wait until I get me hands on ye!" the bloke yells. "I'm going to fuckin' kill ye!"

"Who's that?" I ask Eagle Eye.

"It's your pal Sammy 'The Sleeper' Jenkins," he replies, grinning.

"What the fuck is he doing down there? Jesus Christ. What's the plan here… to bleedin' shoot him?"

"No, I'm going teach you how to use this thing," he says, touching the rifle. Another puff of vape smoke covers his face. "Go ahead, look what's in the scope."

"Ye bleedin' wankers. When I find out who you are, yer dead!" Sammy shouts, losing his voice.

I take a peek into the scope. I see Sammy squirming below on a wooden board.

"Are those balloons around him?"

"Sure are," Eagle Eye says. "I want you to shoot them."

"I'm going to miss."

"You won't. And if you do . . ." He shrugs his shoulders. I look back in the scope again. The rifle feels foreign. I aim at a pink balloon. It hangs from a nail like a testicle.

My right eye is a bit blurry. I quickly squeeze the trigger. It fires, making an explosive firecracker sound. I miss the balloon by a foot.

"Jaysus," Eagle Eye says. "Maybe you shouldn't have your hands on a sniper."

"Feck off."

Simone comes running up the steps, sitting next to me, panting.

I close my eyes. My face, ribs, and throat are still sore. I take a breather, trying to relax. I open my eyes, then calmly press the trigger again. Everything feels like it's in slow motion as the bullet leaves the chamber. I can feel its ferocity, its power. The bullet hits the pink balloon, exploding beside Sammy's head.

"Ah Jaysus. Me bleedin' ear. I can't hear anything!" he screams. I go again, hitting a blue balloon beside his hip. I'm on a roll. I hit a red one, then a purple one. The last one is green, right between his legs.

I never heard a grown man cry like this before. Behind me Eagle Eye is recording the incident on his phone. Simone barks. She sniffs the bullet shells. We walk down the stairs. Sammy is moving his head from side to side. His skin is soaking wet.

"I think we should just finish him," I say jokingly.

"Yeah, throw him in the Liffey," Eagle Eye suggests.

"You know what, I know a fella who owns a furnace. We can dump him in there and watch his flesh and bones melt."

"That would be a lovely show. I'll bring the popcorn."

"I'll give ye anything," Sammy cries. "Please don't kill me, please!"

"I don't know," I say to him. "You've been a right prick this past year."

"I won't hurt anyone else," he pleads, tears rolling down through his blindfold.

"He doesn't care about the public, the rules of society," Eagle Eye says. "How to respect your elders. We need to put some manners on him."

"I agree." I get closer to him. "Listen up. I want an apology video from you today for all the shit you've done this year, and if you don't have one by three o'clock, I'll torture your mother, I will make her cry and bleed before I kill her. You fuckin' hear me?" He doesn't respond. "Are ye deaf?"

"Yes! Yes! I'll have the video out today, I swear." The dog sniffs his toes. "What's that? Who's touching my feet?"

"Good."

We leave the building, dumping Sammy 'The Sleeper' Jenkins out on the street, still tied up and blindfolded. He runs so fast barefoot that he nearly gets hit by a tram.

Eagle Eye asks, "Were you serious about throwing him into a furnace to watch his flesh and bones melt?"

"See you soon, Eagle Eye," I say. "Send me over that recording of Sammy squealing when you get the chance."

When I arrive back in Smithfield Square, music is playing and people are hovering outside the Cobblestone pub, drinking and singing. Simone starts moaning.

"What's wrong, love?" I pet her down and make sure her collar isn't too tight.

"Hi," someone says. I look up and Olivia is standing in front of me. Her smile sinks my heart down to my stomach.

"I thought we were supposed to meet up later," I say, stammering out my words. Simone jumps up on Olivia's knees, fretting for her.

"I couldn't wait, so I thought I would drop over to see if you were around."

"She misses you," I say.

"I miss her too."

We both stare into each other's eyes. "Let's go somewhere less noisy," she suggests.

All three of us end up in a café next door to the Light House Cinema. The atmosphere is calm inside. We order two lattes and two blueberry muffins.

"What happened to your chin?" I ask her.

"I bought an electric scooter last week. I ended up falling off it yesterday and scraping my chin on the road."

"Those things are a nuisance," I say.

"How did we end up like this?"

"I don't have a clue," I say, nabbing a piece of the muffin with my fingertips. I take a deep breath and exhale. "Remember I said I used to work in a chipper in my twenties?" Olivia nods. "Well, I did that for years. I would scrub the disgusting floors every single day. I absolutely hated it. And this is while I was hooked on pills. So, I applied for a new job at a family-run pub as a doorman. I didn't see it as just a pub. The family who took me in treated me well. During this time, I met Jack Magee, who owns the bike shop. He means a lot to me. You could say he's like a father figure. What I'm trying to say is that it's hard to give up these people in my life after all these years."

"So, you're choosing them over me, is that it?" she says.

"No, no, I'm not saying that at all."

"What are you trying to say? Because it sounds like you're making excuses again."

"It's not like that, Olivia. I'll quit my job and find something else, I swear. Just give me time to make a bit of money first," I say, almost whispering my words, gently touching her hand. Her lips tighten up, almost turning white.

"I'm not waiting around for you to get your shit together." She stands up, her hand slipping away from mine. "You could get yourself killed. How many times have you come back home hurt?" Olivia's eyes start watering. She still cares about me, even knowing what I do.

"I don't want to lose you." I stand up too. "Please, just give me time."

"I can't... I just can't." Olivia clenches her fists. I wonder. Is she going to punch me? Headbutt me?

She doesn't do either one. Instead, she turns and hurries out of the café.

I try to follow her, but the leash gets tangled between my legs and I stumble.

"Olivia!" I shout. I hear the desperation in my voice. So can she. She stops, half outside the door, and turns to look at me. "I need time, please, I'm begging you."

Her fists unclench, just a little.

"Six months, Patrick. Find me then, and we'll see what happens. I can't guarantee where I'll be in my life ... or who I will be." Olivia walks out into the square. I don't have it in me, physically or mentally, to chase after her. What would I say to her if I did?

She turns the corner and is gone.

The rain comes pouring down, but the crowd is still rowdy outside the Cobblestone pub. My heart is beating fast and my body is aching. I sit down and remove the pill bottle from my fanny pack.

The bottle is empty. I stare hard at it in my hand, not knowing what to do next.

I guess I'll start by living with the pain.

OLIVIA'S VISIT

ABOUT THE AUTHOR

Keith Bruton is a writer from Dublin, Ireland. He studied at Technological University Dublin receiving a Bachelor of Science degree in Business and Management in 2014. He lived in Toronto, Canada for four years. He currently resides in Dublin with his partner.

Made in the USA
Monee, IL
18 May 2024

58318381R00139